The Torment of Mr. Gully

THE
TORMENT
OF MR. GULLY

Stories of
the Supernatural

J. CLARKE

HENRY HOLT AND COMPANY • NEW YORK

Published by Henry Holt and Company, Inc.,
115 West 18th Street, New York, New York 10011.
Published in Canada by Fitzhenry & Whiteside Limited,
195 Allstate Parkway, Markham, Ontario L3R 4T8.
Originally published in Australia in 1989 in a slightly different form under the title
The Boy on the Lake by the University of Queensland Press.

The lines of poetry in "The Cuckoo Bird" are from "Spells," by
James Reeves (*The Wandering Moon*, Heinemann: © James Reeves.
Reprinted by permission of the James Reeves Estate).

Library of Congress Cataloging-in-Publication Data
Clarke, Judith.
The torment of Mr. Gully : stories of the supernatural /
by J. Clarke.
Rev. ed. of: The boy on the lake. c1989.
Summary: A collection of eleven short stories
on supernatural themes.
ISBN 0-8050-1421-7
1. Fantastic fiction.   2. Children's stories, Australian.
[1. Supernatural—Fiction.   2. Short stories.]   I. Clarke, Judith.
Boy on the lake.   II. Title.
PZ7.C55365To   1990
[Fic]—dc20   90-34122

Henry Holt books are available at special discounts
for bulk purchases for sales promotions, premiums,
fund-raising, or educational use. Special editions
or book excerpts can also be created to specification.

For details contact:
Special Sales Director
Henry Holt and Company, Inc.
115 West 18th Street
New York, New York 10011

First American Edition

Printed in the United States of America
Recognizing the importance of preserving
the written word, Henry Holt and Company, Inc.,
by policy, prints all of its first editions
on acid-free paper. ∞

1   3   5   7   9   10   8   6   4   2

Contents

The Torment of Mr. Gully

The Cuckoo Bird

When I came in from school, Lotte was standing up on the sofa again, staring at the picture on the wall. *Saint Malo* it was called; the name was written in tiny squiggly letters in the lower right-hand corner, just below the signature.

I put my arms round my little sister and lifted her down onto my lap, but she didn't hug me or put her face up for a kiss; she just kept staring over my shoulder at Saint Malo. "Ha," she said in her thick baby voice. "Ha."

"Yes, it's a house, Lotte," I replied. "A pretty white house with a big green garden. But you wouldn't want to live there. You like it here, with me. With Amy. A-my." But she wouldn't say my name, though she could, sometimes. "Ha," she repeated. "Ha."

"Amy dear," my mother called from the kitchen. "Can you come in here for a minute and help me slice the beans for tea? I'm a bit behindhand tonight."

"I'll bring Lotte," I said. "She can sit in her highchair and watch."

But Lotte began to whimper when I tried to take her out of the room, and my mother told me to leave her there.

"She's been grizzling all afternoon," she added. "That's why I'm so late with everything—she must be cutting a new tooth, though there's nothing there that I can see."

So I settled Lotte down on the rug with her building blocks and her favorite doll, Susan, though I knew she wouldn't play with them; she hadn't bothered with her toys for ages. When I'd finished the beans and laid the table in the dining room, I hurried back to Lotte. She'd been so quiet, I thought she must have fallen asleep, but no: There she was again, up on the sofa, staring at Saint Malo, enchanted.

I knew how she felt. When I was about her age, I'd been fascinated by that picture too. Fascinated, and then, after the nightmare, afraid. Now I just felt indifferent. It was a painting of a house and garden: a big white house with a red-tiled roof and wrought-iron balconies, standing among tall green palm trees. There was a pebbly path leading away from the terrace down into the garden; beside the path was a low stone wall, and though you couldn't see it, you knew that behind the wall, far down, was the sea. And you knew too that it was summer in the garden, hot and quiet and perfectly still, with the scents of flowers and leaves and grasses baking in the sun, and inside the house everyone would be asleep.

Except for the little girl. She was in the garden, in a dark place way down at the end of the path, standing quietly by herself, gazing out in front of her as if she were waiting for somebody. She looked just like Lotte, very small and slightly plump, with fuzzy silver-blond hair and blue eyes. I'd looked like that too when I was Lotte's age, before I'd grown skinny and my hair had darkened. But the likeness between Lotte and the little girl was more exact, their faces very similar: the same pointed chin and small, full-lipped mouth, the same deep blue eyes. There was only one difference, really: The little girl in the picture had a dimple in her cheek, just at one side of her mouth. I didn't care for it; I thought it gave her a sly expression.

"Lotte," I said.

She didn't hear me, or if she did, she took no notice at all.

"Lotte—" I took her by the shoulders and turned her around to face me. "Would you like to play a game? Will we get the tea set and have a party for poor Susan? I think she's feeling lonely."

Lotte twitched her shoulder out of my grasp and began to grizzle. My mother appeared in the doorway, a fluffy pink towel hung over her arm. "Don't start her off again, *please*, Amy," she said. "It's time for her bath." She clapped her hands. "Come along, Lotte—bath time!"

Lotte squealed. She held on to the arm of the sofa and kicked her legs. "No nonsense now," said my mother firmly, dodging the flailing feet. Hauling Lotte up into her arms, she carried her off to the bathroom, and there my little sister's cries were drowned in the rush of the cold tap and the roar of the gas heater.

I shared my bedroom with Lotte. I'd done so ever since she was one year old and learned to sleep through the night. I didn't mind sharing at all; my room was big, with three long windows, and I liked waking up at night and hearing my sister's soft, gentle breathing in the cot beside the door. But that night when I woke, her breathing sounded very different: faster and less gentle, so I knew she was lying awake.

"Lotte," I whispered. "Lotte." She didn't answer, and I got out of bed and tiptoed over to the cot. I could see her quite clearly: There was a streetlight in front of our

house, and the curtains were thin and transparent. Lotte
was lying quietly beneath the eiderdown, her eyes wide
open, staring at the ceiling.

"Lotte," I whispered again. "Are you okay?"

She was really too young to answer me. My parents said
Lotte was a slow talker, just as I had been—all the same,
I thought she'd smile at me or try to say my name. Or she
might say "Ha" again, because I could tell somehow, from
her soft, dreamy expression, that she was thinking about
Saint Malo again.

I used to do that too; I'd lie in my cot, the same one
Lotte had now, and I'd imagine I was inside the painting,
in the garden at Saint Malo, walking along the pebbly path
toward the end of the garden and the dark place where the
little girl was waiting for me. It was all so real that I'd feel
the sun beating down through my hair and smell the grasses
baking and hear the sea tumbling softly on the other side
of the stone wall.

But Lotte didn't say "Ha," or "A-my." Instead, she
opened her small, full-lipped mouth and a whole sentence
came sliding out.

"I can cheat strangers with never a word—"

How frightened I was! Lotte couldn't talk like that: She
couldn't say a whole sentence. She didn't know words like
"cheat" and "strangers."

"Lotte!" I cried, hoping, though even this was scary
enough, that I'd imagined it and she hadn't really spoken
at all. She smiled then, but not at me; she didn't even seem
to see me, or know that I was there. She sighed and closed
her eyes, and in a moment she was asleep. I went back to
my bed and pulled the covers close up around my face. *"I
can cheat strangers with never a word."* . . . You see, I *knew*
that sentence. It used to repeat itself in my head, over and

over, back in the days when I thought about Saint Malo all the time, about walking slowly along the path above the sea. And now that I was older, I saw how queer it was that I should have repeated a sentence like that, when I was only two, and slow at talking, just like Lotte.

I suppose you can never really be sure what little kids think inside their heads, or what they know. Just because they can't talk doesn't mean they don't know words: It's just that they can't make the sounds. Perhaps my mother had read a poem to me when I was a baby, and the words had caught in my head like scraps of paper on the thorns of a blackberry bush. I knew them—I just couldn't say them. And the same thing had happened with Lotte: Mum must have read the poem to her, and it had stuck in her mind. She'd *spoken* the words though, out loud—I puzzled over this for a few minutes, and then I suddenly had an answer. I'm not very good at math; I hate it, and when I'm doing homework problems, my head goes around and around and I can't think, but sometimes I'll wake up in the middle of the night and I'll see the answer to a sum I've struggled with for ages—all at once, just like that—and in the morning I'll have forgotten again; I couldn't do that sum if you offered me a million dollars. Perhaps Lotte's talking was like that—night talking.

I settled down to sleep, hoping I wouldn't have my nightmare. It was the nightmare that had put me off Saint Malo, made me hate it so much that for a while I'd closed my eyes whenever I passed through the room where the picture hung.

I'd dreamed that I was inside the painting, just as I'd wanted to be, walking along the path toward the place where the little girl should have been standing. Only I couldn't see her: There was just this dark place, an emptiness, a *hole*, where she should have been. And Saint Malo wasn't at all like I'd imagined from outside. It was quiet and still, but it wasn't a hot summer's day—there was no smell of flowers and leaves and grass, no soft sound of the sea. It was cold, terribly cold, like it might be if you were locked up inside a refrigerator with the door pressing up close against your face, shutting out the light. The very air felt solid, as if it were turning into rock, and big leaves brushed against my face. As I approached the center of the empty place where the little girl should have been, I caught sight of the faint outline of her dress, and the lighter glimmer of her hair, just in front of me. She turned and smiled at me slyly, and I saw her face close, a face almost exactly like mine, except for the dimple. She was moving away from me, out of the picture, away from Saint Malo.

She was leaving me there! And all at once I knew what the little girl intended; she wanted to live in my house: to sleep in my bed and eat off my bunny plate, to sit on my father's lap and have my mother kiss her good night. I wouldn't let her do it! I reached out and caught at her dress. I pulled and pulled with all my strength, dragging her back into that dark empty space where she belonged. Then I woke up in my cot, cold all over, and after that I never looked at Saint Malo, not for a long time, and when I did, I found it didn't interest me anymore. It was just a picture hanging up on the wall.

At breakfast the next morning I asked my mother if she ever read poetry to Lotte.

"Sometimes," she answered.

"Does she like it?"

"I guess so—she likes being read to. Or she used to. She's gone off it a bit now."

"Did you ever read her a poem that goes: 'I cheat strangers with never a word'?"

"I don't remember. I could have, though it doesn't ring a bell. Did you have it in school?"

"Yes," I lied. I didn't want to tell her I'd heard Lotte repeat the line; she'd never believe me anyway.

"It sounds rather a creepy poem, just from that line," my mother remarked. "I don't think I'd have read it to Lotte."

"Mum?"

"Yes?"

"Where did Saint Malo come from?"

"Saint Malo?"

"That picture on the wall in the living room—it's called Saint Malo."

"Is it? I never noticed." She roused my father from his newspaper. "Did you, Tom?"

"Can't say I did."

"It's written at the bottom."

"We bought it just after we were married," said my mother. "We saw it in the window of a little antique shop— more of a junk shop, I suppose—and we fell in love with it. With the little girl, really—we wanted to have a little girl who looked just like that. And the amazing thing was, we did. You were just like her when you were little."

"So's Lotte."

"Yes, she is. *Two* little girls—it's almost like magic, the likeness is so exact."

"Except Lotte and I don't have dimples."

"What?"

"That girl in the picture has a dimple in her cheek. I think it's creepy, like a hole in her face."

"Oh." My mother put her head on one side, consideringly. "I think dimples are rather nice, especially in children."

"Where was the shop?"

"I don't think it would be there now, Amy. It's almost fourteen years ago, and the place didn't look as if it was doing much business even then."

"But where was it?"

"It was down behind Neasden Parade, in that narrow street that runs down toward the park," said my father. "The last shop, I think, or the second last. There was a queer old chap who ran the place—remember him, Ruth? His eye?" My mother gave a little scream. "She remembers," Dad grinned.

"What was wrong with his eye?"

"It was glass, I think. It never moved; he always seemed to be looking at you."

"Now there's something much more creepy than a dimple," smiled my mother. "A glass eye."

I didn't agree.

That afternoon I skipped my music lesson and hurried down Neasden Parade toward the narrow street my father had mentioned. Franklin Lane it was called, and I walked up and down twice, but there was no antique shop, no junk shop; it seemed that my mother had been right. No little man with a glass eye. I was rather relieved. I didn't know what I'd really been looking for anyway: Perhaps I'd hoped to find another Saint Malo, stacked up in a dusty corner. For if there was another one, even lots of them, then our Saint Malo wouldn't be so special: I wouldn't have that queer feeling that it had somehow been *meant* for us—for my mother and father and Lotte and me.

The last shop was a greengrocer's and the second last

was a bookshop. I went in there—I liked bookshops, and this one was new and glossy, with stacks of fresh books piled up on the tables.

"Do you have any poetry books?" I asked the young man behind the counter. He was a boy, really, not much older than me, and as I looked more closely, I saw that it was Heck Summers, who'd been at our school last year.

"Nursery rhymes, you mean?" he grinned.

I tossed my head. He thought he could tease me because he was out of school and I was still in it.

"No," I said firmly. "Proper poetry."

"Oh, *proper* poetry, is it?" He grinned again, and jerked his head toward the back of the shop. "Over there, bottom shelf. Not much call for your poetry, I'm afraid."

I searched along the shelf—the books were dusty, even a bit creased here and there, as if the people who occasionally browsed through them never had enough money to buy. I found Lotte's poem at last, in a book of children's verse. "Spells" it was called.

> *I can cheat strangers with never a word.*
> *This is the spell of the cuckoo bird.*

"What do you think this means?" I asked Heck Summers, who had come prowling up behind me. He took the book in his big freckled hand and read the lines slowly, a puzzled expression on his face. "It's a riddle of some kind," he said at last. "I'm not much good at that kind of thing: It's like crosswords—you've got to have the knack. Don't know much about cuckoos, except: Don't they chuck baby birds out of the nest, and take over?"

I stared at him.

"Funny, isn't it," he said, "how the parent birds feed the cuckoo—they don't seem to know their own babies are gone."

I nodded dumbly.

"Cheer up," he grinned. "It's only a poem, after all."

Suddenly I liked him—he was so familiar and ordinary, with his freckles and striped shirt and the little gold earring he wore in one ear. I didn't like poems and pictures: They were disturbing, dangerous, and as I walked home, I made a list in my head of all the things I saw that were ordinary and familiar and safe: the fish-and-chips shop on the corner, kids on skateboards, Evan Duncan on his newspaper round, old Mr. Manning putting his bins out on the curb.

"Shh," warned my mother as I came into the kitchen. "Lotte's sick."

"What's wrong with her?"

"Oh, nothing much. Don't look so worried. It's just a virus—one of those twenty-four-hour ones, the doctor says. He's given her some tablets, and I've just got her off to sleep. She had me worried this morning, though—she was lying on the sofa, limp as a rag doll; when I picked her up, her head wobbled."

I shivered. "But she's all right now?"

"Oh, yes. The doctor says she'll be fine in the morning. But if she wakes up in the night, come and tell us right away, won't you, Amy?"

"Yes."

"I wonder—I wonder if I should move her cot in with us, just for tonight."

"Oh, don't do that," I said. "I don't mind if she wakes me."

She hesitated. "Just to be sure—"

"But the doctor said she'd be all right, and if you move her now, she'll wake up."

I felt Lotte would be better with me; I knew what was

wrong with her. I'd keep awake all night and watch over her.

I didn't. Sometime after two I fell asleep, and when I woke, there was silence in the room. I turned the light on. It wouldn't wake her—I could tell she wasn't there.

I knew where she was, of course.

But there was no small figure standing on the sofa beneath Saint Malo: The picture hung dark and square on the wall, and Lotte wasn't there.

"A-my," sang a voice from the corner of the room.

"A-my." I flicked on the lamp: There was my sister, sitting on the rug, nursing Susan on her lap, stroking the doll's raggy yellow hair.

"Oh, Lotte!" I pounced on her and held her tight. "You frightened me—I thought you'd gone forever!" How cold she was! "You shouldn't be here, out of bed," I scolded. "You've been sick." All the same, I was glad to see her with her doll; it meant she was forgetting about the picture. Perhaps she'd had the same nightmare I'd had, long ago— that was what might have made her sick.

I bundled her up in my arms and carried her back to our room. "Dal," she murmured, still stroking Susan's hair, and then, in a firmer, clearer voice: "Mine."

"Yes, she's yours. Of course she is." I pulled the eiderdown around her, tucking Susan in as well. "Now Susie can get warm too." I put out my hand to the lamp switch, and Lotte looked up at me and smiled. In that instant, just before the light went out, I saw the dimple in her cheek, deep and immeasurably sly. "Lotte!" I cried.

But my sister wasn't there anymore. She was back in the living room, in that dark garden hung up on the wall, small and cold behind her wall of glass. In Lotte's bed, beneath the covers, clutching Susan, the cuckoo slept.

The Boy on the Lake

That summer my parents went to a conference in Berlin. I'd hate it, my mother told me—Berlin was a dreary city at the best of times, and January was the very heart of winter. "You'd be stuck in a hotel room with nothing to do," she said. "You'd be bored, and you'd miss the summer here." As she spoke the word "summer," my mother came up close and put her arm around me, and moved her other hand toward the window and the garden outside. "The summer is so beautiful here," she whispered. "You wouldn't want to miss it."

Then my father came into the room. He was a tall, thin man, rather stooped, though he wasn't old. He worried about me, though I could never figure out why. Every evening when he came home, he'd say as he walked in the door, "Where's Jonas?" There was real anxiety in his voice, as though he expected to hear that I'd gone, vanished. Sometimes in the middle of the night I would wake to find him standing by my bed, watching as if I were a baby. And yet on the weekends when we were home together he hardly spoke to me: He seemed shy.

I hoped that day he would say I could come to Berlin

after all; I knew he wouldn't want me to be left behind. But my mother shook her head at him, and he said slowly, "You'd better stay, Jonas."

"But where will I go?" I cried. "Where will I go when you've gone?"

My father looked down at his feet. My mother turned from the window and glanced scornfully in his direction. Her voice had a stubborn sound. "You'll be staying with your aunt Nelly," she said firmly. "Remember Talli Balli?"

I didn't. I knew I'd been there, years and years ago when I was hardly more than a baby, but I couldn't really remember the place or the people. Talli Balli was out west, and small—you could find it on a map, but the map had to be big, the kind that puts in every tank and dam, every water hole and railway siding and rusty shack beside a crossroad.

Aunt Nelly was my mother's older sister. A long time back, when she was only seventeen, Aunt Nelly had run away to the bush and married a shearer called Jack—that was how she'd ended up living in Talli Balli. There was a photograph of her in an old box my mother kept in the drawer of her dressing table. The box had a rich scent to it, sandalwood, I think. The photograph was in sepia, and whenever my mother took it out and looked into its old brown world, she always frowned. Once she said, "Nelly was always very pretty—beautiful, really." Her voice sounded sad when she spoke the words "pretty" and "beautiful," and I knew this was because she herself had never been like that: At least, not when she was young and it counted. She'd been a scrawny kid with freckles and rat-tailed hair, while Aunt Nelly was plump and blond and laughing and her face took your breath away.

So when I saw my aunt standing on the siding at Talli

Balli, I had a shock. She wasn't beautiful like she'd been in the photograph; she wasn't large and laughing and generous. She'd changed: shrunk down into a sharp-eyed stick lady in a garish floral dress, her skinny legs as pale and straight as matches. Her hair was gray and straggly, her nose curved like a parrot's beak, and her eyes glinted like chips of mica in a stony curb.

Uncle Jack was the big one, a huge lubbocky man with straw-colored hair and a broad, rosy face. He looked simple and open, like the pictures in children's books: a farmer or a woodcutter or a harmless, genial giant. Standing on the siding with the moonlit country lying quiet all around us, a shiver ran through me. Although I hadn't been able to recall that early visit to Talli Balli, I'd expected when I saw my aunt and uncle that I would suddenly remember them.

But I didn't: No memories stirred when I saw their faces, nor when I entered their little house with the three rooms and the wide verandah all around. They might have been strangers. The idea troubled me through my first days in Talli Balli: I kept waking up in the tail end of the night, just before the birds began, and I'd go cold all over, thinking how the wrong people had come to the station to fetch me. Just in that hour, with the thick, silent dark outside, it seemed utterly true. But in the daylight I saw this certainty for what it was: a little kid's fear of being taken away by the fairies. There was no reason to suspect my uncle and aunt. Of course my aunt would have changed; thirty years had passed since the photograph in my mother's box had been taken. And I'd been a baby on that last visit; babies don't remember people's faces. They had the right names, after all: the people in Talli Balli called them Nelly and Jack, and their surname, Finney, was printed on the mailbox by the gate. They were okay.

All the same, it was unpleasant living in that house. Uncle Jack was quiet—he could sit for hours on a wooden chair drawn up to the kitchen table, softly smiling to himself and occasionally reaching into his shirt pocket for the makings of a cigarette—but my aunt's temper was as sharp as her face. Some of its force was directed at Talli Balli. She hated the place. "A hole in the ground," she called it, or a "god-forsaken dump," and when she spoke these phrases, her voice was so bitter and miserable that I felt my heart sink. But her real fury was directed at Uncle Jack; she couldn't stand the sight of him. The mornings, in particular, were bad.

She wouldn't let him have butter on his toast at breakfast. When he reached out for the flat green glass dish (my mother had one just like it in the cabinet at home and the sight of it here always comforted me), Aunt Nelly wrenched it from his grasp with one tiny hand and with the other sent the margarine tub skimming across the table. "That'll do for the likes of you," she hissed. Uncle Jack didn't seem to mind: he went on chewing placidly at his square of toast, apparently indifferent to what was spread upon it. He'd shake his head and even grin in my direction, as if inviting me to share a coward's admiration of his wife's brave spirit.

After breakfast he'd head off in the truck toward the outlying stations. Looking for work, I supposed, lining up a job for the shearing season. On my second morning at Talli Balli he'd offered to take me with him on his rounds. Already bored, I'd jumped at the chance. But Aunt Nelly put her foot down. "Never," she'd pronounced, her face set and grim, and those fierce bright eyes had raked her burly husband, slashed him through from top to toe. Uncle Jack had merely grinned and shrugged, turned from us and ambled off toward his truck. Standing by the letterbox, I watched him disappear along the red road, thick dust billowing up behind him.

It was bad again at dusk when he returned, for Aunt Nelly often locked the door against him. Guiltily, safe inside, I listened to his slow footsteps, queerly light for so big a man, creeping around the verandah; I heard his clumsy hands fumbling at the window sashes, and sometimes, with that same painful sinking of the heart I felt when I heard my aunt speak of Talli Balli, I made out a whimper from the verandah: a painful, baffled, beaten sound. If he found every cranny stopped against him, then Uncle Jack settled patiently outside, like a dog on a doormat, to wait for a change in Aunt Nelly's mood.

She liked *me*, I could see that easily enough. It wasn't just that I was allowed to use butter at breakfast and was never locked outside; her affection showed itself in other small ways. She worried that I might be bored, and dug out for me some yellowed books that she said had once belonged to my grandfather. She'd written to my mother, years back, and asked for them to be sent on. Why? I wondered. Had she been homesick? Had she planned to have children? I wondered again when she showed me the battered black bicycle in the shed behind the chicken coop: It looked like a kid's one, though a kid from long ago. "Long ago and far away"—that was a song my mother used to sing to me when I was little, and in a sudden flash I saw her face, with the dark hair curling around her cheeks, as it did when there was rain in the air. The vision confused me utterly: What was I doing here, in a place where I didn't belong, with people I didn't know? Why was I standing in a dusty yard in a place called Talli Balli while a witchlike old woman offered me a rusty bike? At home in the garage

I had a new French racer, and I had a mother who was elegant and beautiful, even if she had once been a scrawny child. It was as if I'd been given away. I stared blankly at Aunt Nelly.

" . . . just needs a drop of oil," she was saying. "Then you can ride into the town in the mornings, before the heat gets a go on—buy yourself some lollies if you like." And she reached into the pocket of her ugly flowered dress and drew out a crumpled five-dollar note.

"Thanks," I muttered, a bit ashamed of myself. I wondered guiltily if my parents were paying for my stay; my aunt and uncle didn't seem very well off. And Aunt Nelly was all right—she couldn't help being bad tempered, it was living in a place like Talli Balli that did it, a place she loathed. And with a man she seemed to hate. I thought that so much hate might make you go all small and sharp and ugly.

"But don't go near the lake," she warned.

It was a warning I'd heard many times before. Whenever Aunt Nelly went out, to visit a crony in the township or to attend a meeting of the CWA in Colong, she always called me to her and, gazing straight into my eyes, repeated: "Don't go near the lake."

"Why?" I'd ask.

She'd open her mouth as if to speak, but no words came out. There'd be a faraway expression in her eyes, as if she was searching for an exact and perfect answer—one that would convince me utterly. Then she would give up. Her eyes would sharpen, and she'd say something quite ordinary: "It's deep. It goes straight down."

"How deep?"

"Never you mind. Deep enough for you, my boy. You

mustn't ever go swimming there. People have gotten lost."

Lost? The word seemed queer. Surely she meant drowned.

"I won't," I assured her. "I can't swim."

"All the more reason." She looked at me consideringly, and, I thought, with relief. "Why can't you swim?"

It was a reasonable question; everyone asked it. I was the only kid in my class who couldn't swim. There were just three of us in the school—freaks. "I don't like the water going over my head," I replied. "I hate it in my eyes and ears, shutting things out: It's like being dead."

She didn't smile, the way everyone else did. "Just keep away," she repeated. "It's a bad place."

She warned me also against Uncle Jack. "If he comes back early, before I do, if you're ever alone with him, don't listen to a word he says. Don't take a spot of notice."

I nodded dumbly. I didn't really understand what she meant, for Uncle Jack seemed harmless enough. I supposed the warning had something to do with the way she seemed to hate him: Perhaps she didn't want me to find out he was nice, to like him and become his friend. Then she would be left out.

She needn't have worried about my listening to Uncle Jack's side of the story: I was having a lot of trouble getting the hang of his accent. It was a soft, flat, country one where the words seemed to run all together; I could hardly make out anything he said. It was a source of hot embarrassment to me, for my camp bed was made up in the lounge room, and on those nights when he was not locked outside, and after Aunt Nelly was asleep, Uncle Jack would creep into the room and sit smoking by the empty grate. He talked to me then—his voice rambled on, soft, friendly, confiding: he might have been recounting the events of his day out at the sheds on White Plain or Kurrajong, he might have been lamenting Aunt Nelly's hard way with him, or even cravenly apologizing for her—I had no way of knowing. I dreaded those moments when his voice rose a little and then paused, for I knew he was asking a question, and worse, that he expected some answer. I couldn't stay silent; I wanted him to like me—much more, I wanted him to know that I liked him. Guilt hung heavily on me: guilt about the butter and the locked doors. I wanted to show that I had no part in Aunt Nelly's treatment of him. I did not want the butter—lately I had taken to saying that I preferred margarine—and I did not lock the door. But I could hardly understand a word he said.

"What did you say?" I kept asking. It was hopeless, a pointless question, for when he repeated the sentence, I still couldn't make it out. "What?" I said again, mortified that he might think me deaf, or stupid. After a few nights I became wiser, replying to that questioning rise of his voice with a vague "Hmm" that could have meant either "yes" or "no." He seemed satisfied, and gradually, as he came night after night to sit by the grate, I began to understand him a little. At first I made out a word here and there, then whole phrases and even sentences began to loom like shapes through the mist, on the very edge of my understanding.

"Amed few," he murmured. . . . I puzzled for a few seconds and then suddenly *heard:* he was saying "A mate for you." He had found me a friend—someone to play with!

"Who?" I asked eagerly.

But he raised a finger to his lips, and his flat, gray eyes slid sideways. Turning my head in that direction, I saw Aunt Nelly standing in the doorway. She didn't speak at all, but fixed her husband with those mica eyes and slowly,

like a big, tame bear, Uncle Jack got to his feet and shambled across the room toward the door. As he passed her,
she drew aside a little; her bony little figure seemed to
twitch all over with dislike. She waited a moment, tense
and alert, until the creak of the screen door and those odd,
light footsteps on the verandah told us that Uncle Jack was
well out of earshot. Then she flew in a rush to my bedside.

"How long has he been coming in here?" she demanded.
The eyes flashed, bony fingers clutched at my pajama shirt.

"I don't remember," I muttered. "Not long."

"What has he been saying to you? What does he talk
about?"

"Nothing," I mumbled.

"Nothing?"

"He talks—he talks quite a bit—but I can't understand
what he's saying—I can't follow his accent."

The bony fingers relaxed. She stood back from me,
smaller than ever in the shadowy room. Her nightdress was
pink and frilly like a child's. "But if you get to understand,"
she said slowly, "then remember what I told you."

"What was that?"

"Don't *listen* to him. Don't take a speck of notice. You
hear?"

"Yes," I whispered, pulling the blankets up over my
head. When I drew them down a moment later and peeped
out, my aunt was gone. The little house, three rooms and
a verandah on the edge of nowhere, was silent.

It was dull in Talli Balli, a flat, painful dullness like nagging toothache. There were no other kids in the township.
Aunt Nelly said all the young people had moved down to
the city years back; there was nothing for them here.
They'd found work in the city and settled there, bought

houses and raised families and never came back, except for Christmas.

A dreamy look came suddenly into her eyes. "Kids," she said softly. And then, "I never had any, you know."

I nodded.

The softness vanished and a spasm of anger flitted over her face. "Not with him the way he is."

I didn't reply, for what could I say? I hated it when she railed against Uncle Jack; the bitterness in her voice caused a curious, itchy little wave to pass across my scalp. I flinched as she added grimly, "Not for him—not for him to give away."

The phrase frightened me; it had been in my head for a long while. Who, I wondered, would give away their children? Surely not Uncle Jack; he was too soft and placid. Even the idea was cruel. *Given away*—I pulled back from it, and though the room was stuffy with the heat of late morning, I shivered as if someone had walked over my grave.

The days were long with no one to talk to, and those afternoons when Aunt Nelly went over to Colong seemed endless. I'd always thought people who talked about being lonely were soppy or sorry for themselves, but now I kept hearing the word in my head, and I saw that it sounded the way you felt, narrow and hollow and empty, like a used cigar tube. I roamed the little house; shamelessly I pried in drawers and found nothing but clothes and old receipts and empty needle books with rust on their flannel pages.

I leafed through the old books that Aunt Nelly said had belonged to my grandfather: *Treasure Island* and *Kidnapped* and *King Solomon's Mines*. I liked old books; at home I had been a great reader, but here, out on the verandah, sprawled in the cool place beside the tank stand, I found myself reading the same words over and over again, unable to make any sense of them. The light fell dazzlingly on the page—somehow, in this place, it seemed silly to read, and the ideas that were in the books didn't seem worth bothering about.

So I would get out the old black bicycle and ride into the township. There was nothing much there, either: a dusty main street—Reef Road, it was called—a church and a pub and a post office–bank with petrol pumps in the yard outside. The big general store was called Finlays', and beside it there was the smaller shop run by Mrs. Mulletson. A kind of corner store, I suppose; it sold groceries and bread and sweets and the newspapers that came up from the city twice a week. Behind Reef Road were several unmade streets of weatherboard cottages. That was Talli Balli, all of it, laid out bare beneath the sun, like a stale sandwich on an old tin plate.

And yet—I could remember, from when I was small, gazing out of the windows of country trains, and there, just beyond the glass but out of reach, I would see those little roads, narrow as paths, calm and secret in the dusk, snaking away into the land. They seemed mysterious to me then, and private, and I longed, with a yearning that was like heartache, to know where they went.

Now as I rode my bike up the potholed expanse of Reef Road, I *knew:* those secret roads went to places like Talli Balli, dull little towns baking in the dust, places without any beauty or mystery at all.

There was nowhere to go once you got there: I was too young for the pub, and there was nothing in Finlays' to attract me; the windows were full of plaid blankets and hardware and those garish floral dresses Aunt Nelly wore. There was only Mrs. Mulletson's, really, and I always stopped off there to get a can of drink and some sweets. Mrs. Mulletson was plump and blond and always smiling, just like I'd expected Aunt Nelly to be from the photograph in my mother's box. She was, I suppose, about my mother's age, in her forties, and the sweets she sold might have been that age too. They were museum pieces, the kind of sweets my mother might have had as a child, or even my grandmother: rainbow balls and sherbet bags with licorice straws in the top and tiny wafer-thin bars of chocolate in deep purple wrappers. Inside the silver paper the chocolate was white with age and the letters printed on it were wobbly and misshapen where they had melted and set and melted again over many summers.

Even on the first day Mrs. Mulletson knew who I was. She wanted to know how I was getting along at my aunt's place.

"Fine," I replied, and she lowered her powdery lids and looked at me from the pale gray slits beneath. "Have much to do with your uncle?" she inquired.

"He's out all day. I hardly see him at all."

She nodded then, and seemed to relax, lowering her big freckled arms onto the countertop. "There's not much doing in a place like this," she said sympathetically. "Not for a kid your age. What do you do with yourself all day?"

"Oh—read," I answered, and then, thinking that this might mark me out as a bit of a freak, I added quickly, "and ride around on the bike."

"Hard work, that," she laughed. "Rather you than me any day." Then she became serious again. "Don't go near the lake," she warned.

Everyone in Talli Balli said this. My aunt, the women—her friends, I supposed—whom I saw going in and out of Finlays', the old men who sat on the wooden benches outside the pub, yarning and smoking together. There were two benches, one on either side of the door, and I noticed every time I passed how there were always several old men on the right-hand bench, and only one on the left. This solitary old man was ancient. His white hair had a rusty tinge to it as if he'd been a redhead; his skin had blotches that once might have been freckles. He never joined in the conversation of the other old men, though they greeted him as they came and went—Dory, he was called.

"Don't go near the lake," the old men called as I passed. "It's deep," they added. "Goes straight down." Only Dory didn't warn me, just as he never greeted me; yet every time I passed the pub I felt his eyes were on my back.

Slowly, as the hot, dull days passed, the idea of the lake began to fascinate me; I knew I must go there, just to take a look. And then the weather was so hot—a burning, blazing mid-January—that it would seem like a miracle to see water on the land. Perhaps it wasn't there; perhaps the lake was a myth, a tale made up by the old people to give glamour and danger to their dull little town.

The turnoff wasn't far from my aunt and uncle's house; I'd passed it many times on my way into Talli Balli, a narrow, pebbly track between empty paddocks of high, blond, tussocky grass. There was no signpost, but I knew it was the place—Uncle Jack had pointed it out to me that first night as we drove home from the siding. He was the only person in town, apart from Dory, who hadn't warned me not to go there.

As I rattled along the track, the sun blared down on my head and shoulders and I felt a bright pain at the back of my neck, moving upward into my skull. My head filled with the images and colors of coolness, deep blues and greens, trees and soft grasses and water and slender, shivering reeds. Three kilometers in from the road the track rose suddenly, the paddocks fell away, and there, from the crest of a small hillock, I saw the lake for the first time.

It was brown and hard. There were no gentle colors, no reeds or grasses, and the only trees in sight were a clump of scrawny gums just below the hillock. The murky water had no movement in it, and no light; it was flat, brutal, and somehow intrusive, like a great paw thumped down upon the land. The lake was huge: the farther shore was almost invisible, lost in a haze of dust and heat; toward the center was a string of small islands, ugly, rounded humps littered with stones and driftwood.

I propped my bike against one of the scrawny trees and walked down to the water's edge. An old wooden jetty snaked out from the shore—though the wood was gray and old, it seemed solid enough; all the same I trod carefully, remembering the words of my aunt, the ladies outside Finlays', the old men on the pub benches. "Deep," they'd said. "Goes straight down." At the far end I sat and dangled my feet in the lake; it was thick and tepid, like stale bathwater, faintly scummy. A fishy smell rose from its surface. I looked around. There was no litter at all, either in the lake or along its shores; no Coke cans or chip bags or old cigarette packs—either the locals were neat or they heeded their own warnings: No one came here. How far was it to the other side? The haze made it difficult to judge, for although the water was still, the air above it shimmered and rocked with heat. I felt the pain starting up in my skull again and closed my eyes. And there in the dark, unexpectedly, I saw my mother's face again, and now the pain was like grief; as if she was gone and lost to me forever instead of just gone away for a little while. I shook my head and the face vanished. I opened my eyes and saw something moving on the water. Far out, beyond the humped islands, drifting along the line of hidden shore, there was a boy in a boat. Despite the haze he seemed very clear to me; I could make out his face beneath the bright red hair, a clear white face with a sprinkling of freckles across the nose. I could see his eyes; they were gray. I could even make out their expression—a deep seriousness, still and grave.

The boat moved slowly, purposefully, from one end of the lake to the other. What was he doing? I could see no sign of line or net. He wasn't fishing—he seemed to be looking for something. I watched him all that afternoon until the light began to fade and I knew I must go home, and not once, in all that time, had the boy given any sign— a smile, a wave, a shout across the water—that he had seen me. Yet I knew he had; I knew he had seen my face as clearly as I had seen his. I *felt* it, as, passing the pub in Reef Road, I felt Dory's eyes upon my back.

All that night I lay in bed and wondered. Why had no one told me that there was another boy in Talli Balli? No kids, they all said, just like they all said, "Keep away from the lake." Was that the reason? Was it because he rowed on the lake and might take me with him? But why had I seen no sign of him in the township? I had been in Talli Balli more than three weeks; surely, in that time, I should have caught a glimpse of him in Reef Road, in Finlays' or the post office or Mrs. Mulletson's store. And something else niggled at me—the boy's face. How was it that I had seen it so clearly when he was so far away? I hadn't been able to see the farther shore, and yet I could make out the freckles on his nose and that curious, grave expression in his eyes.

The puzzles tormented me. I went every morning to the

lake, and every morning the boy was there, moving up and down, calm and serious, like a grown-up person absorbed in some important business. He made me feel small and ashamed—I was just hanging about, really, looking for company; I wanted, like a kid, to play. The sense of inferiority silenced me. I didn't call out to him; I just sat and watched while the sun beat down on the water and the crows jeered in the spindly gums.

As the days passed, it seemed to me that the boat was coming closer. At first it had been behind the islands; I was almost sure of that, for I could recall the flicker as it slid for a few seconds out of sight. Now it was in front of them, its long, slow movement placid and uninterrupted.

When I was not at the lake, I prowled Reef Road and the small streets behind it, hoping to catch a glimpse of the boy setting out or going home. But he seemed to have no home; whatever time of day I went to the lake, I found him there, and I felt sure that if I came at night I would still see him out there on the water. All night in bed I tossed about, and when I slept, I dreamed of the lake and the boat moving slowly up and down and the boy's white face, which would not turn to me. One morning the dream was so fresh in my head that I spoke out.

"Who is that boy on the lake?" I asked Aunt Nelly.

She was ironing on the kitchen table, and her narrow head shot up like a snake's from grass. "Stay clear of that one, you hear?" she hissed.

"But who is he?"

She didn't answer my question, not right away. She lowered her head over her ironing and a ragged sigh escaped her, an unexpectedly gentle sound. I'd been sure she'd be furious at me for going to the lake; instead, she just seemed sad. I probed, dangerously.

"You said there weren't any children in Talli Balli," I began.

"He's not a child," she answered, eyes still hidden.

"Yes, he is. He's about the same age as me. He's about thirteen."

"It's Dory's grandpa," she whispered.

"What?" Her remark mystified me. Dory was the old man who sat on the bench. How could this boy be his grandpa? Or had she meant grandson? "Do you mean—" I began, but the rage I had anticipated now broke out: Aunt Nelly thumped the iron down on the table with a mighty bang. "You keep away from that one! Stay clear! Do you hear me?"

I was silent.

"Promise!"

"I don't see—"

"Promise!"

"All right," I muttered. "I promise."

Aunt Nelly stared silently into my face for a moment and then, with a little gasp, she fled from the room, as if she knew my promise was a lie. It's easy to lie when you are fascinated by someone, as I was by the red-haired boy. It's easy to tell any old tale, do any wrong thing—nothing matters, except being near.

All the same, some moments later, as I passed along the verandah outside the bedroom window and heard Aunt Nelly crying, I thought I would stay away from the lake. For a little while, anyway.

Instead I went into the township—I thought I might ask someone there. I passed Dory, seated on his bench as usual. He was very, very old, I saw now, of a quite different generation from the other old men. The skin on his face was tight and transparent, his eyes were sunk deep, gazing at nothing. All his friends must be dead, I thought, all gone long ago, and though the town itself wouldn't have changed much, walking its streets he must have felt like a ghost, a person left over. I shivered, and walked on into the comforting closeness of Mrs. Mulletson's store.

"What'll it be for you today?" she asked. "Same as usual?"

I nodded, and she reached into the fridge for a can of lemonade. As she opened it, I asked, "Mrs. Mulletson, you know how you said I must be bored in Talli Balli, with all the kids gone away?"

"Yep."

"Well, there *is* a kid. I've seen him."

She lowered her eyes, poked a straw into the can, and handed it to me.

"On the lake. There's a boy who rows on the lake."

"No, there isn't."

"Yes, there *is*. I asked my aunt."

She tightened her lips. "Your aunt was a fool to say anything. There's no boy. He's just . . . just a mirage. In the heat, like. You think you see him, but you don't, really."

I knew she was lying: Mirages weren't like that. "My aunt says he's called Dory's grandpa. Did she mean grandson? Is he the grandson of that old man who sits outside the pub?"

"Grandson? I told you, he's just a mirage. They call him Dory's grandpa because he's old, old as the hills. Older than Dory even, and he's ninety-two this winter. Always been here, Dory's grandpa has."

I looked her straight in the eye. "He's a real boy, isn't he? Mirages aren't like that—they're just sheets of water, or trees—"

Mrs. Mulletson didn't reply. She stared out of the open doorway, over the roof of Finlays' store. " 'Nother one comin' in," she remarked.

"What?"

"Dust storm. You'd better get off home, son. Don't want to get caught out on the road."

I followed her gaze—I could see no red smudge in the sky, and besides, she was looking east. The storms always blew from the west, blotting out the sun, bathing the land in an eerie red light. She was just trying to get rid of me.

"He's real, isn't he?" I pressed.

Her head, long and flat like a fish's, swiveled toward me. "You keep away from that one. Keep clear, you hear me?" She twitched her shoulder in my direction, as if I was a bluebottle buzzing at her ear. "You get along home now, son. Take your lemonade and go."

I went instead to the lake. He was there, as he always was. I walked out to the end of the jetty and sat down, feet dangling in the brackish water. I planned to stay all afternoon, till dark and after dark, on and on until the hour when the boy came in from the lake; then I would speak to him. That's what I intended, but in some other part of my mind that had nothing to do with plans or answers I knew that the boy would never come into shore, that he didn't go home in the evenings like everyone else.

The idea came to me that he had been sent to the lake as a kind of punishment: he had been left, abandoned, given away. *Given away* . . . as the words formed themselves in my mind, I saw my mother's face again, no longer laughing, but cold and stern like Dory's. She was cruel too: She couldn't be bothered with me, she had left me here in Talli Balli, given me away. And my father had done nothing to stop her. He hadn't said a word.

Hours passed. I must have fallen asleep, and when I woke, the night had come on, moonless black. Yet I could still see the boy out across the water, and for the first time I could sense that he noticed me, was glad I had come. No mere child looking for playmates would come out to the lake at night; I had proved myself to him. My shyness vanished, and standing there by the edge of the dark water I raised my hand and waved, and at once all the sad doggedness of the boy's face broke up in happiness and delight; he turned the boat smoothly and began to glide quietly across the lake toward the jetty.

And then there was a sound behind me: a scatter of footsteps, a harsh panting, a sharp voice calling my name. Aunt Nelly was running along the jetty. I turned toward her and then swiveled back, swiftly, toward the lake. But it was too late—the boat was already far away, heading out toward the islands. I had lost him.

My aunt hurried me home. She had come on foot, though it was at least three kilometers from the house to the lake. Why hadn't she brought the truck? In my head an answer formed itself: because she didn't want Uncle Jack to know. But why not? I couldn't ask her; she'd become very silent, and I felt afraid to disturb her. She never spoke at all, and strode so fast along the track that she made a small funnel of wind beside her, and the long dry grasses moaned and rustled as we passed.

When I woke the next morning, the house was so still I knew it must be empty. I wandered through all the rooms and around the verandah toward the backyard. To my surprise I saw Uncle Jack there, leaning against the post by the back gate, easy and smiling to himself. As I stepped down from the verandah, my nose wrinkled: There was an unpleasant smell in the air, fishy and dank, like the smell that hovered above the lake. I peered around the yard. There was no sign of my aunt; Uncle Jack was alone.

"Gonna be another scorcher," he remarked, jerking his tawny head toward the coppery sky. I noticed that his voice seemed clearer out of doors; I could make out every word. It might have been the light—most of my conversations with him had taken place at night, when I was in bed. Perhaps it was different when I could see his lips move, or my difficulty in understanding him might have been an illusion, like the time my father lost his glasses and couldn't seem to hear properly.

"Where's Aunt Nelly?" I asked.

He grinned. "Your aunty told me to tell you she's gone off to Colong to do a spot of shopping."

"But it's so early!"

"She wanted to beat the heat. She'll be back by lunchtime." He squatted down against the post and took out his tobacco pouch and papers. I watched him roll the rusty threads flat between his fleshy palms. His skin seemed moist: I supposed it was sweat, yet it gave me an impression of cold, like the shine on a frog's skin. I didn't like him as much as I had when I first came; he was too soft, and there was something sly about him. He looked up at me, grinning still. "He's all right, you know," he said.

"Who?"

"Dory's grandpa. He's a friend of mine."

"Honest?"

"A real old friend. From a long way back."

"Aunt Nelly doesn't seem to like him."

"Oh—" Uncle Jack smiled, shrugged briefly. "You know your aunty. A bit of a loner. There's lots of people she don't like—and who don't like her."

I pondered this. I could imagine my aunt's bitter spirit scaring people off, and yet she did seem to have friends: those ladies who went in and out of Finlays', Mrs. Mulletson. It was Uncle Jack who had no one.

"Does he ever go home?" I asked. "The boy, I mean. Every time I see him, he's on the lake, even at night, and I've never seen him in the town."

"Oh, he goes home all right, when he's got a feed."

"A feed?"

Uncle Jack shot his head back and made a brief, unpleasant snapping motion with his jaws. "Grub, you know—chow."

"Is that what he's doing on the lake, then—fishing? He doesn't seem to have a line or anything."

"He's looking for a feed," repeated my uncle tonelessly, "like I told you." He made the snapping motion again. "And when he's got it—well, then he goes on home."

"Home? Does he live with that old man, Dory?" Before my uncle could answer, a thought struck me. It was childish, but I spoke it out loud. "Doesn't Dory give him anything to eat?"

Uncle Jack chuckled. "Not him. Not old Dory. He's too sly for that. Catch him feeding *that* boy!" He grinned, rising up from his heels, brushing the dust from his jeans.

"What does he eat?" I blurted idiotically.

"Dory's grandpa? Oh—tender things." The word was unexpected; it wasn't one you thought he'd use.

"Yeah, tender things," he repeated, reaching in his pocket for his car keys. He jerked his head toward the truck parked outside the gate. "Well, I'm off. See ya."

"See ya," I replied.

I went straight inside to the kitchen. From the fridge I removed the remains of last night's chicken, wrapped it in plastic, and shoved it in my pocket.

The boy was waiting at the end of the jetty, the boat held steady against the stumps. I took his hand; it was cold and moist to the touch, and when I felt that chill, I hesitated for a moment. But the sound of footsteps along the jetty spurred me on, and I jumped defiantly into the boat. Revolt rose up in my heart—why shouldn't I go on the lake? The boat seemed sturdy enough. Why shouldn't I have a friend? I was thirteen, old enough to make my own decisions; they had left me alone, given me away, so I would do as I pleased. I turned to tell all this to Aunt Nelly.

But it was Uncle Jack who stood there on the edge of the jetty, gazing down at us, smiling and friendly. "Told ya he was okay," he remarked, nodding at me. "Didn't I? Told ya Dory's grandpa was an old friend of mine."

The red-haired boy smiled, a small smile, with closed lips.

"He's all yours," called Uncle Jack jovially.

The boy dipped his oars into the water, and the boat began to slide across the lake. When I looked back a moment later, my uncle was gone.

Alone with the boy, I felt shy. His silence made me silent too; I felt I didn't know what to say, how to begin a conversation. As we passed the islands, I reached into my pocket and pulled out the parcel of chicken. It was rather squashed. "I brought you something," I said lamely. "Some chicken—in case you were hungry." When he didn't reply, I added, "It's very tender."

We were in the very center of the lake, and the boy

paused in his rowing and raised his eyes to mine. He reached out for the parcel and in one single deft movement took it in his hand and threw it into the water. There was no splash; the brown oily stuff parted and the package slid in. Dory's grandpa smiled; this time he opened his lips, and I saw his teeth. They were odd—small and glistening, slightly pointed, and they seemed to go a long way back in his jaw. There were too many of them, I saw as he came for me, far too many. Sharp as needles they felt, and piercing.

The Dripping Tap

I n September, two months before my final exams, we rented a cottage just out from Winto, a small town in the Mallee. It was quiet and peaceful there, just what we needed, because I had to study and Dad had to finish some writing and Mum, who is a primary-school teacher and was a bit worn out from the long winter term, said she was going to sleep—sleep all afternoon and read trashy novels all night.

We soon fell into a little routine. In the mornings, while I worked, my parents went off for a walk to the town or along the river path; in the afternoons my mother dozed in the bedroom while my father shut himself up in the small room behind the kitchen, from which you could hear the occasional tap of his typewriter and long, long silences that I knew were painful. In the evenings we talked or listened to the radio, and sometimes Mum would go over a problem I was having with history or economics. They were keen on my doing well in the exams and going on to University: I wasn't so sure—I hadn't a clue what I wanted to be. There was only one thing I was certain about: There was no way I'd ever be a teacher or a writer.

So I had the afternoons to myself, and not being a great reader, there was nothing much to do but go walking around the country. I didn't bother with the town; it was a one-street affair that I found depressing (imagine living there!) and the river path bored me after a few days—it was too tame. I'd set off through the back gate and along the narrow rutted track that crossed the grassy wasteland the locals referred to, mysteriously, as "the common," and then straggled on into nowhere. "Nowhere" was rough, hilly scrubland, crossed by dry creek beds and dotted with stunted, twisty trees. It seemed to go on forever, the dry land rising and falling—you'd reach the crown of a hill and expect to find a different landscape on the other side, but it was always the same: more scrub, more dry creek beds, more twisty, twiny trees. There was something very silent about these walks: no sound at all except the crunch of my boots on dry twigs and leaves, and the rasp of my breath; no birds around, not even those crows I heard all morning while I was trying to work, flapping and crying above the cottage. "Bare ruin'd choirs where once the sweet birds sang," as my father might have put it.

One afternoon, after a rough morning with chemistry (there was something dreadfully wrong between me and chemistry), I walked for hours, much farther than usual. I came to a hill that seemed higher than the others, and there, on the other side, there really was something: Off in the distance I could see a windmill and the gray, humped shape of an old, tumbledown house. Or at least I'd thought it was tumbledown. The windmill certainly was: so rusty and tottery you felt the slightest breeze might send it over, and indeed just as I passed a little wind must have sprung up, because the blades began to move slightly, and there was a queer, long mournful sound from it, very like a moan. I gave the thing a wide berth; I didn't want to be decapitated by a mass of rusty iron.

But the house—that was the puzzling thing. The impression of ruin I'd had from the top of the hill must have been some trick of light, of sun and shadow and passing cloud, for close up it was quite respectable: a shabby old weatherboard house with a sloping roof and wide verandah. There were even a few scruffy flowers growing in a rough bed beneath the rusted-out water tank, geraniums and some very prickly rosebushes. A tap dripped by the doorstep. The place was deserted: You could tell from the silence that hung about the yard, thick and deep and solid.

I climbed onto the verandah and peered through the front window. I had the shock of my life: There *was* someone in there, a little girl, about seven, I guessed, with a sharp, white, pointed face and black pigtails tied neatly with red ribbons, seated at a table. As I stared through the dusty glass, amazed, she glanced up and caught sight of me, and, raising her hand, beckoned me in. Without a thought, blankly, I went around the verandah and walked through the front door.

The room where the little girl sat was cheerful and homely: solid, old-fashioned furniture, flowers on the mantelpiece, paintings of big sailing ships hanging round the walls.

"So you've come at last," she greeted me, pouting a bit and tossing her skinny pigtails. "You're late. I've been waiting and waiting. Come on, quickly"—she indicated the empty chair opposite her own—"sit down." There were picture cards in neat little stacks laid out on the table, some kid's game, I guessed, and I was right, for she slid one across to me and said commandingly, "Now we'll play Snap."

So we played Snap. We played it for hours, one game after another, till my head was buzzing and I could hardly make out the pictures on the cards. My bossy companion never seemed to get tired, but then, little kids are like that.

"Let's have a rest," I suggested after the eighth game, or perhaps it was the ninth; I'd lost count.

"No," she replied firmly. "You have to play." There was a big smudge on her cheek, smoky black, as if she'd been messing around the grate, and had washed her hands carefully but forgotten her face. Apart from that smudge, she was the cleanest little girl I'd ever seen: There was a white lacy bib thing on the front of her dress, and I'd swear it was actually *starched*. I wondered where on earth her mother was. The kid seemed too little to be left in the house alone, and the thought of her mother made me suddenly uneasy: What would she think if she came back from town, or wherever she'd gone, and found me here, a complete stranger, practically a grown-up, playing cards with her little girl? She could think anything. I shifted nervously in my straight-backed wooden chair.

"Don't fidget," commanded my playmate.

"Where's your mum?"

"Out near the windmill, waiting for Dadda to come home in the sulky."

"What's a sulky?"

She stared at me in astonishment, and tossed those skinny braids again. "You know very well what it is," she said primly.

"No, I don't. Tell me."

"It's a wooden thing with wheels, and a seat inside. Blondie pulls it, and Dadda drives."

"Oh, a horse and cart." They must be real back-to-the-

earthers, I thought. "You say your mother's out there in
the yard, near the windmill?"

"I *told* you."

I hesitated. I didn't want to make her anxious; on the
other hand, I was beginning to feel a little worried myself.
"I didn't notice her there when I came past," I said casually.

"Well, she was there; she's *always* there," the kid insisted.

I got up from my seat and strolled to the window. I could
see the windmill quite plainly; it wasn't very far from the
house, and I had a clear view of the yard and the flat, dry
scrubland with the rutted track winding away to the hill
from which I'd come. There was no one in sight.

"Come back," ordered my companion. "Come back at
once and play Snap."

I returned to the table, and she dealt me a fresh stack
of cards.

"What's your name?" I asked.

"Emily. Don't talk all the time. You can't concentrate
if you talk."

"Listen, Emily, I can't play much longer, really—it's
getting late and I have to get home to my mum and dad.
It's a long way back."

She laughed—there was a gap in her front teeth; two of
them were missing. "You're too big to have a mum and
dad," she giggled.

"No, really, I mean it, Emily. I've been here all afternoon—"

"It's only *morning;* you've only been here a minute."

I didn't argue; it's no use with little kids: For one thing,
they've got no sense of time, and for another, they always
want to win the argument. I sighed and picked up my cards,
and we played on until it began to get gloomy in the room

and I knew I'd have to go, even if Emily made a fuss. Otherwise my folks would have the cops out. But I felt a bit guilty about leaving her on her own; it would be night soon, and though she was so sharp and bossy, Emily was pretty small. And yet she didn't seem frightened or nervous: She wanted me to stay all right, but not because she was scared—it was just that my company was needed for those endless games of Snap.

"Do you know when your mother's coming back?" I asked.

"I told you," she replied. "She's here."

An idea occurred to me: Her mother might be asleep somewhere in the back of the house, worn out with games of Snap. There was a woman in our street at home, Mrs. Curtis, who used to give her little kid a dollar if she'd play quietly and let her mother sleep in the afternoon. Perhaps Emily's mother used this trick.

"Is she asleep?" I asked.

"She's out at the windmill. I *told* you, I told you and told you—you're stupid! You're the stupidest man I've ever met!" After this outburst she fell silent, gazing at me consideringly, and when she spoke again her voice was softer and less sharp. "You can go if you promise to come back tomorrow," she said slyly.

"I don't know about that, Emily. I've got lots of work to do. I'm studying for exams."

"Promise," she urged me.

I hesitated.

"If you don't promise, I'll call my mother: I'll tell her you were mean to me, I'll tell her you pulled my hair. She's got an awful temper, she has big black eyes that flash out sparks, and she'll—"

"Oh, all right," I agreed hastily. Beneath my irritation I

felt sorry for Emily. She must be lonely; the house was miles from anywhere.

"Good-bye, then," she said, quaintly offering me her hand across the table. I shook it gently.

"Be sure you come back now," she called as I went toward the door. "You promised."

"Oh, sure. I never break a promise."

As I passed the windmill, I looked around for Emily's mother, but the place was just as deserted as before, and that thick, solid silence had fallen like a blanket the moment I stepped outside the house. The woman would have to be inside somewhere; no one would stay out this late with a small child alone at home. She must be asleep, really sound asleep. Probably took Valium.

Reaching the top of the hill, I glanced back: Although twilight was gathering, the house was still in darkness, its windows unlighted, and from the rise, once again, it appeared tumbledown, a ruin. Uneasily I turned home.

That evening after dinner (spaghetti cheese: my mother seemed to think she could feed us stuff on holidays that we'd never eat in term time) my father asked me what I'd done with myself all afternoon.

"I found an old house," I replied, but I left out the rest. I didn't feel like mentioning Emily.

"Oh?" he said. "Where?"

"Out the back of the common, miles away into the scrub. It's a queer place; from a distance it looks old, a real wreck, but when you get up close it's quite decent, really."

My mother looked thoughtful. "That must be the old Tanner place. I don't know what you mean by decent, though: It hasn't been lived in for ages. The place must be falling apart by now."

"It's not too bad," I replied evasively. "Do you know anything about it? Who's living there?" She was a great one for picking up bits and pieces of local gossip.

"*Lived* there, you mean. I told you, it's been abandoned for ages."

I didn't contradict her. The locals were obviously having her on for some reason. The house was certainly lived in, I knew that, and I guessed some sharp real-estate agent had done it up and rented it out as a holiday place for townees. That dress Emily wore, for instance, with the lace bib—it was just the kind of gear some of my father's phony friends dressed their little daughters in, getting them up like characters from a book of fairy tales. And the horse and cart, or sulky, as Emily called it; that fitted too.

"What else do they say about it?" I asked cautiously. "I suppose it's haunted or something?"

"Why, did you see a ghost?" asked my father sharply. He wasn't joking; he was interested in that sort of thing.

"No, course not."

"It's not haunted," said my mother. "At least, they didn't say anything like that." She screwed up her eyes thoughtfully. . . ."But something rather awful did happen there, ages back—"

"Seventy years ago," my father put in. "The house has been empty ever since, so I don't see how you could possibly have thought it was habitable." A familiar and irritating curiosity shone in his eyes. "Are you sure you—"

I shrugged, heading him off. "Probably a trick of light. You get some odd light effects around here." I turned to my mother. "What happened there, exactly?"

"Oh, the usual kind of horror story: The farmer who owned the place had gone into town, leaving his wife and child back at the farm—when he came back, they were dead, murdered. The child, a little girl I think, was in the house; the mother was—"

"Out beside the windmill," I supplied.

"Windmill?" asked my father alertly. "Did you see a windmill there?"

"Nope—just joking. A windmill seemed appropriately sinister."

"They didn't say anything about a windmill," said my mother doubtfully. "I got the impression the woman was inside the house as well. They never found the killer. They figured it must have been some out-of-towner: a tramp, a wanderer of some kind."

The story unnerved me, though I didn't believe it for a minute. "Sounds like a typical yarn for the tourists," I remarked, hiding my unease.

"You're probably right," my mother agreed. "Wherever there's an old house, an abandoned place, stories like that grow up over the years and people begin to forget what really happened. It's quite likely the place was abandoned for some ordinary, practical reason: bad land, no water, something of the kind."

"What did you say their name was?" I asked. "The family who lived there, I mean."

"Tanner," she replied.

"We might go out and take a look at it tomorrow," suggested my father. "Where did you say it was, exactly, Cam?"

This was what I'd expected. He was like that, always had been; you'd find something interesting, and he'd take it over, make it his discovery, push you aside. The old house and Emily were my find. I didn't want him nosing about, not until I'd had time to get back, make sure what was going on.

"Miles away," I informed him discouragingly. "Way past the common. I wouldn't go there if I were you; the scrub is full of snakes."

That would put him off nicely; both he and my mother were scared stiff of snakes. That's why they always took their walks into town or along the riverbank, where the ground was clear.

"Oh," gasped my mother. "Do be careful, Cam. You shouldn't—"

I thrust out my feet, clad in the long leather boots I wore for walking. "Have to be a sharp-toothed snake to get through these," I remarked.

"All the same—"

"We could take the car," my father suggested.

"Track's full of potholes," I told him. "You'd break an axle for sure."

"Oh, well, in that case—" He shrugged, but I could tell from the gleam in his eye that he hadn't given up on the idea. He'd put it off for a while, though, probably go into town and buy himself a pair of snake-proof boots. In the meantime, I'd get there first.

The story had bothered me. The characters were right, after all: the mother and child alone in the house and the father off somewhere in his sulky, but all the same I couldn't quite believe it. I knew that kid couldn't be a ghost: ghosts don't play Snap. And there were other things: her hand, for instance. When she'd held it out to me, that hand had been warm and living; ghosts were always cold. And that gap in her teeth, that was *real*, and the smudge on her cheek—a ghost's skin, or whatever they had, wouldn't take a smudge like that. A ghost couldn't get dirty.

When I came to the rise, I stared eagerly in the direction

of the house; I think I had some faint suspicion it wouldn't be there. But it was, quite solid, though from a distance, again, it seemed a ruin. I planned to keep my eyes firmly fixed on it as I walked along the track, to note at what point it began to change, to appear, as it did close up, an ordinary, shabby, weatherboard house. But I forgot; my attention wandered, thinking about Emily and wondering if her mother would be there, and I'd reached the windmill before I remembered what I'd meant to do. Once again, as I passed, a breeze sprang up and the rusty blades turned slowly and that curious, miserable moaning filled the air. I shivered: Now, *that* I could believe, something happening to the mother, just there on that spot. But it couldn't have, or Emily wouldn't have been there in the house.

But was she? Nervously, I made my way to the verandah and glanced through the window. Yes, she was seated at the table again, the little stacks of cards set out ready, waiting for me, I guessed. There was no sign of anyone else around, and once again, glimpsing me through the window, Emily beckoned.

"So you've come at last," she said as I walked into the room. "You're late. I've been waiting and waiting." She spoke naturally enough, in her rather sulky voice, but the repetition of her sentences, the same ones she'd spoken yesterday, set my skin prickling.

"Sorry," I muttered, taking my place at the table. "I had to do some work first."

"My daddy does work," she remarked, and I felt relieved by this variation in the conversation. Just for a moment I'd had the frightening thought that Emily would keep on saying exactly the same things she'd said the day before.

As it turned out, my relief was short lived. We played a

few games—well, quite a number, I imagine, my mind wasn't really on counting—and then, beyond the slip-slap of the cards upon the table, I became aware of a small sound, a sound I'd heard yesterday and hadn't really registered: the drip of the tap beside the front step. That tap—how could it drip? The house was on tank water, like all the houses around Winto, and I'd noticed both yesterday and today that the tank outside was old and rusted, so rusted that its floor was completely gone. There could be no water. Yet the tap dripped.

I turned to Emily. "Mummy out again, is she?" I asked, my voice shaking a little.

"She's not out. She's just at the windmill, waiting for Dadda to come home in the sulky."

I stared at her, terrified. She was wearing the same dress, its lacy bib front still spotless and freshly starched, and on her face the smudge still showed, the smudge that should have been washed off at night when she had her bath before bed, like other little girls.

"What's your name?" I asked.

"Emily."

"Yes, I know that, you told me yesterday, I meant—"

She interrupted me. "No, I didn't. You weren't here yesterday."

"I was," I cried. "I was here all afternoon, playing Snap with you."

"No, you were *not*. I was out yesterday with Mumma and Dadda: we went over to the Wilkinsons' place in the sulky. I wore my new dress; it's a plaid dress, red and green, with black-velvet ribbons down the bodice."

"Show me," I said. "Show me your new dress."

For a dreadful idea had crept into my mind: I'd never

once seen Emily move from her chair. She never fidgeted or got up and messed about like other kids. Even when she saw a stranger peering through the window, Emily stayed in her chair and beckoned him in: Little kids don't beckon, they rush to the door, they call for their mums, and when you're inside they follow you about and sometimes climb all over you.

"Show me the dress, Emily."

She lowered her eyes and dealt out a fresh stack of cards. "I don't want to," she whispered.

"I don't believe you've got one—I don't believe you've got a red-and-green plaid dress with black ribbons down the bodice."

She didn't answer; she just went on dealing out the cards. I was right, then; she couldn't move from the chair. Emily was fixed there, imprisoned forever in the last moment of her life, which was always morning, a morning when she had been seated in this room playing Snap at the table.

Alone?

Or with a stranger? While her mother waited outside by the windmill, fixed there in her place, forever waiting for Dadda to come home in the sulky.

"What's your name?" I asked hoarsely.

"Emily."

"Your second name."

"It's Tanner," she answered proudly, lifting her head. "Emily—Louisa—Tanner."

I rose unsteadily from my chair. "I've got to go," I said. "And no stopping me." I moved quickly toward the door. Emily Louisa Tanner sat in her chair and screamed.

"I'll tell my mother on you! I'll tell her you won't play with me. I'll tell her you're bad—wicked. I'll say you hurt me. I'll say you tortured me—she's got a terrible temper: She'll get you, you can't get away, she'll come after you and she'll chop off your head. Ma-ma! Ma-ma!"

I burst out of the door and raced across the yard, past the senseless dripping tap, the windmill, clattering and moaning once more in the wind, up the rutted track, stumbling in the potholes. Once at the rise I didn't look back, but pushed on through the scrub, my chest heaving with terror and sheer effort. The morning breeze had turned into a strong wind: Dust and small, sharp twigs flew about in the air; the twisted trees writhed and bent toward the earth. Halfway home I paused for breath. Furtively, fearfully, I glanced back along the track in the direction I'd come from. I half expected to see a figure hurrying after me, a tall lady in a long, old-fashioned dress, black eyes flashing with fury—Emily's mother. But there was no one.

It was getting dark. Why was that? When I'd left home this morning, it had been just after eleven. I'd set off early in case Dad came back with his snake-proof boots and suggested we take a walk to the old house. I wished now I'd waited. And surely I hadn't been long in Emily's place— no more than an hour. I glanced at my watch: four o'clock, later than I'd thought, but far too early for the dark to be coming on. I shaded my eyes against the dust and looked back toward the horizon, roughly in the direction of Emily's house, along the track curving and winding across the creek beds. There, in front of the sun, blotting it out, I saw a long, whirling spiral, twisting and turning, heading now to right and now to left, but always, inexorably, moving in my direction. A cyclone, a huge one, so strong it had gathered up branches and tree trunks and sheets of iron. I stood quite still, for I didn't know which way to run, and as it came closer, an immense and solid funnel, roaring and moaning with a sound that had something human and familiar about it, I saw what was in its center.

The windmill!

As I watched, frozen, the thing approached the track some fifty meters behind me and began its dreadful pursuit. I ran then, stumbling and dragging myself upright again, struggling on, the terrible moaning full in my ears. I knew now what it was, *who* it was, and I knew what she, Emily's mother, intended to do: I had no doubt of it. Emily had warned me, and the line of the old nursery rhyme sounded like a madman's refrain in my head:

> *Here comes the candle to light you to bed,*
> *And here comes the chopper to chop off your head.*

Two lights appeared in the gloom ahead of me. Headlights—a car, lurching and rattling with a solid, familiar sound. My father!

The car stopped and I rushed toward it. "Hurry!" I screamed, clawing at the door, wrenching it open, tumbling inside. "Turn the car around, quick!"

My father wrenched at the wheel, the car began to turn, and he stared backward, dazedly, through the rear window.

"Hurry!" I screamed again, but he kept on looking out there. "It's going," he said wonderingly. "Going off the other way. That's queer—the wind must have changed." His voice shook. "I thought we were goners there for a minute."

I followed his gaze: he was right. She *was* going, whirling over the scrubland again, westward, moaning and crying, hurrying back home to Emily.

I saw my father's scared face in the gloom. How glad I was to see him, how glad his infernal curiosity, his poking and prying and taking things over, had sent him after me.

"Let's get out of here," I urged. "She— it might come back."

For once he didn't argue, didn't ask me who "she" was, didn't *talk*, and we sped back through the lightening country, toward home.

The Shutter

When I was sixteen, halfway through form five, something queer happened to me. I suddenly lost sight of everything, went blind—not in my eyes, for I could still see, but inside my head, where I thought and felt about the world. It was like a shade coming down, the wooden shutter type you find sometimes in old country trains: the kind that *clamps* shut. *Clamps*. When I hear that word, even now, I have an image of Mrs. Levitt's face, the way she looked at me when I refused to draw the picture for her. Clamped.

I don't like things that are screwed up tight, shut fast. In form two there was this boy in our class, Tony Coady, who was knocked down by a car. We went to see him at the funeral parlor, and except for a tiny scratch on his cheek there was no mark on him. He was just the same, except that he looked—he looked as if he was in a vice. Mrs. Levitt had that look about her. . . .

But it was long before I met Mrs. Levitt that the shutter came down in my head and everything seemed far away and nothing had any point to it. I didn't care anymore if it was Monday or Friday. I didn't count off the days of term like everyone else did, marking off September and October and November till good old December and the long summer holidays came rolling around. I couldn't be bothered hanging around the corner store with the other kids after school or going off to the game on Saturdays. I didn't even care who won the Grand Final. When my friends came knocking on the door, I got my mother to say I was out. I told her I had homework to do. She couldn't believe her luck, seeing me go into my room every afternoon and shut the door without even being told.

But I was doing nothing in that room—just lying on the bed, staring at the ceiling. Or sleeping—I did a lot of sleeping in those days, and I didn't much like waking up. It frightened me, waking up and finding nothing in my head, and nothing in the day to interest me, so I'd close my eyes and burrow down into the pillow again. And then my kid sister Polly would come and tug at the edge of the eiderdown.

That was the only reason I got up at all, because I didn't want Polly to think I was a dag. She was much younger than me, only four, and she was a really pretty kid. But it wasn't just the prettiness you noticed—she had something else, a kind of spirit, I suppose you'd call it, that made her seem more alive than other kids, as if she were a picture drawn with gold pencil and they were just sketches done in ordinary old lead. You felt she was the kind of person who'd do something great when she was grown up. She was special, not like anyone else; not ordinary, like me.

And after the shutter came down, Polly was the only person I could still care about, and when I saw her or thought about her it seemed to lift a little, and a corner of light shone. But only for a moment.

So I pretended a bit, for Polly's sake. I got up and went

to school, at least. And that was how they found out about me—there, at school—when I lost interest in my work. Of course that wasn't unusual; in form five lots of kids lost interest in their work. But I went one step further: I stopped doing it altogether. I took no notes in class, I did no home-work, I read nothing. And of course when the exams came around, I failed every subject, even Biology 1, which no one ever fails. I hid my report card, and then the letter that came from the school; but the coordinator rang up and it all came out. I went to bed and stayed there.

My mother took me to the doctor. She and my father were ordinary, decent, dull people who always behaved exactly like the parents in primary-school readers. They even dressed like that; my mother had a blue dress with white spots on it, exactly like Mrs. Jones in *Fay and Don at the Farm*. They were like nice, pleasant robots, very simply programmed, and it used to frighten me to think I might grow up to be the same.

The doctor was a queer sort of fellow, long and lean and so pale he was almost transparent, like a strap of taffy pulled out thin to the breaking point. He didn't seem at home in his surgery; he wandered nervously about, fiddling with filing cards and pens and instruments and making little whispery noises under his breath. As he examined me his hands were shaking, and when he'd finished he stood there for a moment or two with his eyes closed, thinking deeply.

"A rest," he said finally. "He needs a rest. Say, um, till the holidays. Let him stay home from school."

My mother screwed her eyes up small, the way she does when she can't understand someone and doesn't like to say so. "A rest?" she queried. "What from?"

"Oh," he muttered unwillingly, rocking back gently on his heels. "Just, um, er, growing up."

The way he stood there by the window, rocking, with his long white fingers thrust beneath his braces, flipping the elastic, I could tell he felt sorry for me; even sad. Perhaps he thought I was a mental case, but didn't like to say so right out. Perhaps he was one himself.

My mother took his advice and I stayed home. It was awful. I felt like nothing, lying in front of the television watching *Days of Our Lives* and *General Hospital*, and I began to understand all those articles that keep appearing in the newspapers on housebound women. Even Polly went out: off to kindergarten in the mornings, to her friends' houses to play in the afternoon. She had heaps of friends—everyone loved Polly.

It's funny how, when your mind goes empty, some little worry can creep in and take hold, like ivy growing on a dead tree. I began to be anxious about Polly: Whenever she was out, I was afraid something would happen to her. I started being afraid right from the moment she went out the door with my mother, and if they were five minutes late coming back, I'd go and stand by the gate, waiting for the car to come up the hill, my heart jerking up and down like a road-mender's drill through concrete. It got so bad, I hated Polly going anywhere, because I knew that then I'd have to spend that wretched time by the gate, waiting and being afraid. I was even glad when she caught the flu, because it meant she had to stay safe in bed for a few days.

Yet the waiting was never really long—never more than ten minutes or so because, as you'd expect, my mother was a very punctual woman. All the same, those ten minutes always seemed like a whole little life passing by in my head, a useless, boring life, all torment and worry, and all about nothing, because in some lost part of my brain I knew all the time that Polly was safe. The worry wasn't a real feeling, not like the ones I used to have before the shutter came down; it was made up, somehow.

One day they really were late, by some forty minutes, and I went to pieces. I felt sure they were dead, killed in a car crash—or at least that Polly was dead; my mother had probably escaped, to be a comfort to my father in his grief.

No one had died, of course—they'd just stopped off at the library, but by the time they came in through the front door, I was weeping on the best velvet sofa in the living room.

"What's the matter?" cried my mother. She was frightened; she didn't like unexpected scenes. I didn't explain; it would have sounded queer and frightened her more. I just said I had a headache. That was ordinary enough; everyone got headaches.

But I could tell she didn't quite believe me. And from that time she began to watch me. She'd tiptoe to the door of my room and knock, a timid knock that somehow made me hate her. "All right in there?" she'd call, and slide her silly curly head around the edge of the door. At night she and my father talked about me—they whispered, but bits of conversation came through the wall.

"Needs a hobby," I heard my father grumble. A hobby! The very word was old-fashioned; no one had hobbies anymore.

"It's a pity he gave up his drawing," my mother sighed.

She didn't get an answer. I guessed my father had fallen asleep; he wasn't a great one for conversation in the evenings: Being an accountant seemed to tire him out. My mother never learned; I heard her dimwit voice through the wall, persisting. "Remember the drawings, Arthur?"

My father snored like a fat man in a film.

"Remember the drawings?"

I remembered. The memory was sharp and sudden, because I'd forgotten for so long. For once my mother was right—I *had* liked drawing when I was a kid. More than *liked*—it was a kind of passion with me. I'd filled up sketchbook after sketchbook with trees and flowers and houses and cats and dogs and people's faces. Then suddenly I'd stopped. I don't know why; it was just a phase, I guess, just something kids go through and leave behind.

Now the memory gave me an idea: the idea of a disguise. I had to get better quickly, or at least *seem* as though I was better. Otherwise my parents might start thinking I was off my head; they might even have me put away. And I didn't want Polly to think she had a nut case for a brother. I had to look normal; and I had to get out of the house. I was sick of hanging around the gate worrying every time she went out.

So the next morning at breakfast, when my mother started up her pathetic conversation about hobbies and said what a great pity it was that I'd given up my drawing, I played along.

"It's funny you should mention it," I chimed in eagerly. "I've been thinking of taking up sketching again."

You should have seen my mother's face—rosy as the dahlias my father grew down by the back fence! Poor thing, she gleamed all over with relief. I was taking an interest in something!

When Polly went off to kinder I wandered down to the stationery shop on High Street and bought a big sketchbook and a box of pastels. And that afternoon and every day after, I set off around the neighborhood in my artist's disguise, with my pad and pastels and a packed lunch, so that I wouldn't have to come home till dusk. I did draw a little, but I found I'd lost the feeling for it; mostly I just wandered along the streets. But the disguise worked with my family: My parents stopped whispering at night, and my mother no longer walked on tiptoe in the house or listened outside my door. And Polly—well, Polly still liked me; I guess she would have anyway, even if I'd been a nut case locked up behind a wire fence.

It felt strange walking around the suburb in the middle of the day, when everyone else was at school or work. The streets were empty and the houses still as stones thrown down inside their gardens. Those houses looked as if no one lived inside, or as if a spell had been cast and everyone sent off to sleep for a hundred years. But I knew this was just how it was in our neighborhood in the middle of the day. Quiet.

The last time I'd been through these streets at this quiet time was way back when I was a kid of Polly's age; and I thought that if I finished school and got a job like my father, then the next time I'd walk here like this would be when I was an old, old man. It was a scary idea; I didn't want to think about it.

All around these streets I kept seeing things I hadn't really noticed for years: the disused tennis court at the bottom of Francis Street, with the weeds breaking in clumps through the hard, red earth; the little concrete corner store over on Marloe Avenue, run by a pair of twins, middle-aged men who still dressed identically, as if they'd made some promise to their mother on her deathbed. And there was the funny house on Loome Street. When had I last seen it? It must have been years back, for I hadn't been up Loome Street since I was friends with Harry Austen, back in grade three. Yet the memory seemed fresher than that, as though I'd seen the place just yesterday. Perhaps I'd often dreamed about it, in those queer dreams you don't remember when you wake, though their landscape stays on in your head like the memory of another world.

The house was old; you saw that at once, for it was made of wood and there weren't many wooden houses left in our neighborhood. It was painted a deep, dull shade of gray all over, without any trim or relief, and it stood on a very narrow block squeezed in between the Austens' house and the Brennans'. There were old-fashioned shades on all the windows, cloth shades with silk tassels, and they were all pulled tight down to the bottom of the glass so you couldn't see inside at all. There was no verandah; the front door opened out straight onto a big square of stone paving, shaded by the ugliest tree I've ever seen. It was huge and gray; the bark reminded me of a wrinkled elephant's hide; the branches twisted outward in weird, contorted shapes, and there were no leaves at all, only thick clusters of waxy white buds. It was a magnolia; I think my aunt in Leeton had one growing in her back garden, though hers was smaller and less ugly. The tree made the whole yard dark and oppressive, yet beneath its branches someone had set out a bright new redwood table and bench, as if they thought it a pleasant place to sit.

Looking back, I can almost swear that the redwood bench was always empty when I passed by on my wanderings; and yet, on the afternoon when I first saw Mrs. Levitt seated beneath the tree, I felt just as I had about the house—that she had always been sitting there, and that I knew her well. Because of this I stared a little as I passed, and so she noticed me.

"Hullo," she cried, and though she was old, her voice had a childish note. It quivered in the air after she'd spoken, like an arrow shot into a tree.

"Hullo," I answered. I slowed my steps a little, but I

didn't stop walking. The truth was I felt uneasy. Not because of the feeling that I'd seen her before—no, it was more like plain embarrassment. I was afraid she might be a bit like old Mr. Leary, who lived in the house next to the school. He was lonely and he stood in his front garden most of the day, pretending to rake the lawn but really, as every one of us kids knew, just waiting for someone to come past so he could get up a bit of conversation. He talked on and on, really fast, so you knew he needed the talking badly. It's strange how, when you know people want something badly, you feel like staying away from them, as if they had some kind of disease. All the kids crossed to school on the corner so we wouldn't get caught by Mr. Leary.

At first I thought Mrs. Levitt might be like this. She was an old lady, and the house had a bare look about it that suggested no one else lived inside.

"Out sketching?" she called, nodding toward the pad under my arm.

I nodded back.

"You must show me sometime," she said softly. "One day when you've nothing at all to do." And then she turned away quite casually toward a row of potted plants set beside the front door, as if she was wondering whether they needed watering. I hadn't seen the potted plants before—they were new, and for a moment I had the feeling that, like the redwood bench and table, which looked so out of place in the dark garden, they were stage props of some kind.

When Mrs. Levitt turned away from me like that, so casually, as if she had plenty of other things on her mind and didn't really care whether I came back or not, I felt reassured: She didn't need me; unlike Mr. Leary, she wouldn't keep me there, talking on and on. And then, the easy, untroubled way she said "One day when you've nothing at all to do" seemed to hint that she knew how I felt, understood about the kind of emptiness that was inside my head, and wasn't scared silly like my mother.

So I went back, though I can't remember making the decision. I can't remember anything at all between that day when I first saw her beneath the tree, and another day, much later it must have been; for the magnolia buds had opened into gross pink-rimmed flowers and the little dark garden and the sense of being inside it was old and familiar to me.

There I was, seated on the redwood bench beside her, my sketchbook open on my knee, turning the pages of boring old houses and trees and cats and dogs and flowers, while Mrs. Levitt asked the question she always asked and that I could never bring myself to answer. She wanted to know what I cared about, and she wanted me to draw a picture of it for her to keep inside her house.

"But you *know*," I protested. "You know that's just what's the matter with me. You know there's nothing I care about. You know I *can't* care anymore."

"And that's good, isn't it?" said Mrs. Levitt encouragingly.

"Good?" I frowned and put my hand up to my forehead, as if I had a headache coming on. I'd told her all about the shutter coming down inside my head, and at first I'd liked it that she took my lack of feeling so carelessly, as if it were quite normal, even better than normal. But gradually I became doubtful, confused—surely it couldn't be *good* not to care, as Mrs. Levitt seemed to think.

"You don't want to be all cluttered up with feelings," she said cheerfully. "You'll never get anything done that way, will you?"

Dumbly I shook my head. I didn't know what she meant at all.

"It's best to be free," she continued pleasantly, and she waved her hand in the direction of her dark gray house with its blind, shuttered windows.

"Free," I repeated idiotically, staring at the house, which looked like a prison to me. And while I was puzzling and dithering she slid the same old question in again, only this time she made it sound like a fact, a fact to which I must agree. "I think there's something you *still* care about," she said slyly.

For some reason I didn't want to mention Polly to her. What I felt for my sister was private, deep inside, the only real thing left to me. I didn't want to tell it.

"There is something, isn't there?" purred Mrs. Levitt, moving a little closer to me on the redwood bench. I drew away; for the first time I could feel some kind of need coming out of her; she wanted something badly. The hair on the back of my neck began to prickle; a little shiver ran beneath my skin.

"Relax," she said softly. "You're too tense. Breathe deep—"

I took a deep slow breath and at once the color blue came into my head, flooded in like morning through the windows, and with it a warm feeling of peace. Blue. And suddenly I remembered the book, a book my mother used to read to me when I was a kid. An old book that had belonged to her own mother.

"Close your eyes," I heard Mrs. Levitt saying. I closed them—and I could see the book's cover then, the dull blue cloth with a little square picture in the center, fashioned like a window, and through the window you could see a marvelous garden filled with trees and flowers and birds and a little princess walking among them.

I'd loved that book. The funny thing was that I'd lost it; I'd hidden it away in a special place, somewhere safe, and then forgotten the place, like you always do. I'd searched and searched, and when Polly grew old enough for stories, I'd searched again, but I never found the book, and then I'd forgotten all about it.

"Well?" whispered Mrs. Levitt.

"It's—"

"What? Speak up, boy. What do you see?" Her voice sounded sharp, and I flinched. "It's a book, a book my mother used to read to me."

"Oh, that," she said listlessly. "Is that all?"

"*The Juniper Tree,*" I said. "That was its name." And then my hand, of its own accord, began to move across the blank page of my sketchbook, effortlessly drawing in that blue cover, the garden in the window, the princess walking among the trees, until it seemed the book lay there before me on the page, just as I had last seen it.

Mrs. Levitt reached out her hand. "May I have it?" she asked. "To keep?"

For a moment I hesitated, but there seemed no reason why I shouldn't give her the drawing, so I ripped out the page and handed it over. As I rose to go, for it was getting shadowy, Mrs. Levitt said softly, "It's in the old brown suitcase in the basement."

I ran all the way along Loome Street—I wanted to get home quick, to find the brown suitcase, to see if Mrs. Levitt was right and the book was there.

But I was late.

We had a rule in our house: Wherever I was, I had to

be home by five thirty, half an hour before tea at six. It was the same for my father, I suppose, though for him such rules weren't really necessary; he lived the kind of life where he was always, by nature, safe inside them.

"You're late," said my mother as I ran into the kitchen. "Where have you been?"

"Just out sketching," I replied. "Up at the old house on Loome Street. I didn't notice it was getting late." I edged my way to the door, but she put out a hand and stopped me.

"What old house?"

"You know—the gray one with the big tree in the garden. I think it's a magnolia."

"There aren't any magnolia trees around here; it's too cold for them." She put her head on one side and eyed me suspiciously. "Where did you say the house was?"

"Loome Street. Next to the Austens."

"You mean the Brennans' house. It's not old; they built it only the year after ours. And they don't have a magnolia tree."

"No, no, not the Brennans. It's in between—the gray house between the Austens and the Brennans."

She frowned. "There's no house in between," she said. "The Austens and the Brennans live next door to each other."

I paid her no attention—my mother was vague about places; she didn't get out all that much. I was surprised she remembered the Austens and the Brennans. And then, as if she read my thoughts, she put her hand up to her forehead and shook her head slightly. "I must be muddling the houses up," she said.

I nodded, edging quietly out the back door and down the wooden steps to the basement.

It was there, just where Mrs. Levitt had said, in the old brown suitcase under the steps, where I'd hidden it years ago. I should have felt happy—I'd been so eager once to find this book for Polly. But as soon as I touched it, I felt boredom flooding through me like nausea. I didn't care. I dropped the thing from my hands and kicked it viciously across the floor. I didn't want to read the stories to Polly. Why should I? Why should I do anything? As I raised my hand to put out the light, I turned for a moment and looked back at the dusty old volume lying on the floor—it was nothing.

"Did you find it?" asked Mrs. Levitt the next afternoon.

I stared down at the ground. The magnolia flowers were beginning to fall. There was a big one near my foot, fleshy and bruised. "Yes," I replied. "But I didn't like it anymore."

"That's good." She nodded briskly. "It doesn't do to care about things, or even think you care. Such feelings are like litter: They spoil the view."

"No," I said suddenly.

Slowly, she turned her head to face me straight. Her eyes were black, glistening like prunes in syrup. For the first time I noticed that fierce clench of her jaw: her face might have been set in a vice, and I thought of Tony Coady lying dead in the undertaker's parlor.

"That's how it is," she repeated, as if only a fool would argue.

I must have been a fool. "It's because it was only a book," I insisted desperately. "You can't care all that much about a book. It was a baby's book; I grew out of it, that's all. It's not like caring for *people*, not like—"

"People?" Her voice sharpened again, her head whipped back so suddenly that I flinched, but still I went on.

"When you care about a person," I stumbled. "You know—"

Mrs. Levitt shook her head sadly, and her voice grew soft again. "I don't know," she whispered pathetically. "I have no one." She glanced toward the shuttered house. "No one. Tell me how it is. Do you have someone?"

"Well—"

"Yes?"

"Um—"

"Who?" she rapped out, startling me into the reply I'd been holding back.

"Polly."

Mrs. Levitt breathed deeply, and all her slight frame seemed to soften and relax. "Polly," she echoed, smiling.

I hated the name in her mouth.

"Polly," she said again, and her voice lingered caressingly on those two small syllables. "Is she your girlfriend?"

I've always loathed people who thought in this way: that if you liked a girl, then she had to be your girlfriend. Disgust filled me; Mrs. Levitt was stupid after all.

"Polly's my sister," I said coldly. "She's little; she's only four."

"Only four," mused Mrs. Levitt. With a sudden movement she reached toward me, seized my sketchbook, flicked open a new page, and handed it back to me. "There you are then," she said. "There *is* something you care about. Draw your Polly for me."

I hesitated, but she took my hand, with the pastel in it, and placed it on the page. My hand began to draw, smoothly, almost of its own accord, though more slowly than it had when I drew the picture of the book, as if it pulled against a heavy weight.

Polly appeared from the feet upward: the grubby sneakers, the pretty baby legs, the new pleated skirt (Polly was always getting presents), the pink T-shirt that was her favorite, the slender neck, the outline of her face.

"Closer and closer," breathed Mrs. Levitt.

"What?" The remark disturbed me. I looked up—it was dusky in the garden; it was late. My hand faltered and some strange panic overtook me. "I have to go!" I cried. "It's getting dark. My mother will be worried." I shot up from the redwood bench, the sketchbook fell from my lap, Polly's face, featureless and blank, lay on the ground.

Mrs. Levitt bent and picked it up. She dusted the page with her hand and held it out toward me. "Finish it," she said. There was a grinding sound, faint but unmistakable, as her jaw clamped down on the words.

"No," I replied.

Then there was silence, except for a tiny little breeze that had risen suddenly, rattling the fleshy cups of the magnolia flowers. Mrs. Levitt bent her head. I looked down at the poor thin white hair; beneath it the scalp was pink as a baby's. My fear vanished suddenly, and I felt sorry for her. She was just an old lady, she was just lonely, her family must have grown up and gone away.

"I'll come back tomorrow," I whispered.

She looked up into my eyes. "There's only a little bit to finish," she pleaded. "You can be done in a moment."

"There's no light to see!" I cried, and I heard my voice, a scream in the dusk, and saw my hand like a claw snatching the book from her.

As I ran along the streets toward home, all the old anxiety

for Polly came sweeping back—I felt sure she would not be there, certain I would find my mother weeping in the living room, as I had wept when they were late home from the library. My mother was a sensible woman: She would be weeping for something real.

But the living room was empty. My mother was standing by the kitchen sink straining cauliflower through a sieve; its strong, sour smell filled the house. I ran along the hall. Polly's room was a pool of yellow light in which she sat, safe, with a little doll's cupboard made of plastic blocks in her hand.

"See!" she cried, holding it up to me. I took the tacky little thing in my hand and closed my fingers around it. "Safe," I whispered; and "Safe," echoed Polly from the floor.

In bed that night I began feeling ashamed of the way I'd behaved with Mrs. Levitt, shouting and running off like a kid. She'd always been nice to me; she was the only person who'd bothered to try and understand how I felt when the shutter came down, who didn't just write me off as a nerve case, a loser, a kid who failed at school. Why couldn't I have finished the drawing—even given it to her as a gift? Why shouldn't she have a picture of Polly? What harm was there in it? I was being selfish; I just didn't want to share Polly with anyone else. Tomorrow, I promised myself, first thing, I'd finish the picture and take it around to the house.

I was just falling asleep when something woke me. I'd glimpsed a shape out there on the edge of sleep, some image had appeared and vanished before I could grasp its outline. Something that filled me with dread. I lay still, willing the thing back again, trying to summon a clear picture of it in my mind. It had been square—yes, it was a square shape, and smallish: It was (here the object flashed on me whole and clear) the book I'd found in the basement.

But what was there about an old storybook to frighten me so? I lay still again, breathing deeply, letting the thoughts flow gently through my mind. And I knew that it wasn't the book itself, or the picture on the cover, or the stories inside that frightened me—it was how I had felt about it, or rather, how I had ceased to feel, after I had drawn its picture for Mrs. Levitt. It was as if that old book, which I had once loved, had possessed a living spirit, and the spirit had been put out, leaving it dead to me. With a shudder I remembered kicking it across the floor.

What if I should cease to care for Polly? *I* should be dead, put out. Clamped in a vice.

I switched on the bedside lamp. The sketchbook lay open on the desk behind my bed, the desk where, in a different life, I had once done my homework, made out timetables and Christmas present lists, listened to the radio. Seizing the pad, I tore out the unfinished picture and crept out of the room and down the hall with the crumpled ball of paper shut tight in my hand. In the kitchen I took the matches and set it alight in the sink. I stood in the dark and watched it burn away, twisting and flaring and then dwindling to a crinkle of black ash. I turned on the tap and flushed it away.

Then I crept to Polly's room to check on her. She was lying on her side, peacefully asleep, safe, one arm dangling down over the edge of the bed. I lifted that limp arm gently and placed it back beneath the covers. Warmth filled my veins, light came streaming beneath the shutter in my head. I loved her still; she was safe and I was whole.

But all that night I tossed and dreamed of fires, of Mrs. Levitt, alone and helpless, burning in her bed beneath the shuttered windows. Her body flared and twisted like burning paper; it rose and fell and sank down to a mound of gritty black ash. The house burned up, and the magnolia tree and the redwood bench and table beneath it. The fleshy flowers hissed and writhed and spat like living things.

In the early morning I crept out by the back door and ran toward Loome Street. I expected to find ash, or ruin of some kind, but there was nothing. The house had simply vanished, and the land on which it had stood was gone as well. The Austens' house and the Brennans' now stood next to each other, neighbors—as they had always been. For I knew that if I was to go up the white steps of number 27, knock on the door, and ask Mrs. Austen what had become of the house next door, she'd look at me queerly. She'd say, "The Brennans'? It's there—what do you mean?" Just as my mother had said, frowning a little, "There's no house in between."

As I wandered slowly home again, I found that I was touching things with my fingers: the tops of picket fences, the flat metal lips of letterboxes, the bark of trees. I was staring, too, bolt eyed at all those places and objects familiar to me since babyhood: the corner store, the red postbox on the corner, the houses of my school friends . . . I was wondering what else might not really be there.

Disraeli

On certain nights, nights that follow those peculiarly warm days after a sudden thunderstorm, I often wake and hear a sound in the pool next door. It's a slow, even splashing, as if someone is swimming there, taking long, slow turns up and down the pool, up and down, up and down, up and down. Only no one could swim like that, so tirelessly and for so long, hour after hour after hour, without rest or stay: They'd drown. And the pool is empty now anyway. There's only brown sludge at the bottom, and a thick layer of rotting leaves. The house is empty too; the Hamiltons have gone away to live in the country.

I remember when they came—a young couple, my mother said. I was ten then, and a few years earlier I'd have thought the Hamiltons were old, just because they were grown up and married. I'd only recently begun to recognize the gradations of age in grown-up people, and looking up close, as I passed Mr. and Mrs. Hamilton in the street, I could see they *were* young, as my mother had said. The expressions on their faces were always changing: happy or sad or worried or excited—their faces weren't set, like those of older people. I felt pleased with this knowledge of mine, as if it somehow brought me closer to being grown up myself.

"What a pity they don't have children," my mother remarked. "That house is perfect for children." I could see what she meant: It was the prettiest house in our street, built of sparkling white brick, with a blue roof and windowsills, plush green lawns, and, down the back, a flat safe place to play in, with a wooden cubby house and a marvelous, sparkling pool.

The first thing the Hamiltons did when they moved in was to build a safety fence around the pool so little kids wouldn't come wandering in and drown. That fence didn't look quite right to me; although the spaces between the rails were very narrow, I felt sure that when I was little, two or three, just the age the Hamiltons were worried about, I'd have been able to push and slide my way through.

The Hamiltons didn't have a child, but they had a dog called Disraeli, a big black dog of no particular breed, loose-limbed and rangy with a long, slender muzzle, slightly graying, and beautiful, sad brown eyes. In the afternoons, coming home from school, I often met Mrs. Hamilton taking Disraeli for a walk, and when he saw me, he'd come up, wagging his long, plumy tail, and his mouth looked like it was smiling. "Say good afternoon to David, Disraeli," Mrs. Hamilton would say, and Disraeli would sit down gracefully on the pavement and hold his paw out to me. He was a civilized dog, and Mrs. Hamilton was right to be so proud of him.

On sunny days I often saw them on the front lawn together, Mrs. Hamilton reading a book and Disraeli lying there beside her garden chair, his long muzzle sunk between his paws. Whenever she rustled a page, he'd look up with his big eyes, and she'd glance down at him and smile.

Once he got through the fence between our houses and came to visit me; I fed him some biscuits and then he jumped on my bed and watched while I did my homework, just as though he were mine. Mrs. Hamilton came in to fetch him, looking flustered and anxious. "I hope he hasn't been any trouble," she said nervously. I recognized her manner: When I was little, I used to get out and roam about the neighborhood, knocking on people's doors. Ladies gave me cakes and cold drinks, and when my mother found me there, at home in strangers' houses, she looked embarrassed, just like Mrs. Hamilton did now. And she said the same thing: "I hope he hasn't been any trouble."

"Oh no," I answered, just as the ladies had done for me. "It was nice having him."

"Can I have a dog?" I asked my mother.

She explained that dogs were a whole heap of trouble and said I'd have to wait till I was grown up and had a place of my own.

"Dogs stink," said my little brother Si, who was hanging around as usual.

"So do you," I retorted.

He did, too, of football socks and sweaty runners and all the old mud and grass that was always caked thickly on his legs and clothes. He kicked me on the ankle and I punched him on the arm.

"Stop it, you two!" shouted my mother.

One night when we were watching television, there was a knock at the door. It was Mrs. Hamilton and she was crying. "Is Disraeli here?" she asked, snuffling into her handkerchief. She'd lost him; he'd got through the fence

again and wandered off. "We've been searching all afternoon, knocking on people's doors. My husband's been all
the way to Burwood in the car. You see, Disraeli's not used
to being out, he hasn't really got any road sense, he just
runs, and I'm so—"

"We'll find him," I said confidently, "me and my
brother. No worries." I added importantly, "We know the
area, and we've got the big torches from Cubs."

I wasn't bullshitting. I knew we'd find Disraeli, and it
would be fun hunting around the gardens at night. We
figured he hadn't gone far, that he'd have been around in
someone's backyard when the Hamiltons were rushing
around the streets.

We divided up the houses between us and searched all
the yards, and sure enough, he was just up the road at the
Millers' place.

Mrs. Hamilton gave us ten dollars, which was really a lot
in those days. "I couldn't *bear* to think of him as a stray,"
she whispered, "wandering around, getting thin, wondering where we were."

My parents thought the Hamiltons were a bit silly to
make so much fuss about a dog, knocking on people's doors
in the middle of the night and crying. "It's a pity that child
is so long in coming," my mother said.

The Hamiltons were trying to have a baby; they'd been
trying for a long time. They'd had all kinds of tests but
there was nothing wrong, and finally the doctor said it all
had to do with Mrs. Hamilton's job, which he called "high
stress"—she was a teacher at the high school down the
road. I knew this from listening to my mother's conversation.

So Mrs. Hamilton took a leave of absence. She lay resting
on the plush lawn, stretched out, and wearing, for it was

summer, a bright-yellow sunsuit. A straw hat was perched over her face. She looked funny—she was a bit fat—and people laughed at her, and some of them, ladies mostly, were a bit cross, as if they thought she was spoiled.

But it worked. Mrs. Hamilton got pregnant by the end of that summer. The pregnancy made the Hamiltons change toward Disraeli: They worried he might be jealous of the child and do it harm. I thought it silly of them to suspect such a thing about a dog as gentle as Disraeli, but my mother said there'd been a horrible story in the newspaper recently: A big Alsation, a pet, had mauled a new baby, and the baby had died.

The Hamiltons decided to make Disraeli into a yard dog. Yard dog—even the name sounded terrible to me, harsh and somehow *low*. It didn't suit a civilized dog like Disraeli. Mr. Hamilton built a kennel out behind the cubby house and they chained him up at night, and he howled, and when he howled his voice sounded human and somehow *pure*, like sadness on its own.

I couldn't understand it. I couldn't understand Mrs. Hamilton. I kept remembering her proud face when Disraeli shook hands with me, and the way she'd smiled at him in the garden when she was reading, and how she'd cried on the doorstep, thinking he was lost and might become a stray. I couldn't understand how a feeling like that could simply vanish, and carelessness take its place. It was like something in a fairy tale, like bad magic. It frightened me.

"It's cruel," I said. "He can't understand why they're shutting him out."

"He's not a person, David," replied my mother. "Dogs don't have long memories. In a few months Disraeli will have forgotten all about the time he used to live in the house. He'll think the yard is his home. He's just a dog, remember."

I resented this. "He's *like* a person," I said. "You can tell by his eyes that he feels things, and the way he cries at night—it's *like* being human."

"Bull! As if dogs are human!" yelled Si. "How can you be human if you've got four legs instead of two, and fur instead of skin—and a *tail*? And if you can't even talk!"

"How can you be human if you've always got a football jumper on instead of proper clothes, and great big studded boots like *hooves*, and if all you can do is kick and yell?" I replied. "Besides, that's not what I meant."

"What did you mean then, smart-arse?"

"Nothing." I wasn't going to talk to him. It was a waste of breath.

"Nothing," he mimicked, sidling out the door. "Nothing."

I said to my mother, "There's no difference between being cruel to a person and being cruel to a dog. In India there are people who walk around with little brooms wherever they go to sweep the pavement in front of their feet so they won't tread on ants or beetles or any living thing."

"Oh, India," sighed my mother, and added, more sharply, "Don't go on about it, David."

"Can we adopt Disraeli?" I asked. "They don't want him anymore."

"No, we can't. It would look as though we were accusing them of something."

"Well, I *am*. I'm definitely accusing them of something."

As it turned out, the Hamiltons needn't have worried about Disraeli being jealous. He loved the baby from the start, and the Hamiltons, seeing this fondness, became less anxious. When Tabitha—a silly name, I thought it, like a cat's—was big enough to sit outside on her rug, Disraeli lay a little way off on the lawn, as if he was guarding her. Later, when she learned to crawl on the flat, level part of the yard around the back, he followed her at a respectful distance. The look on his face was foolish and adoring; I didn't like to see it. I didn't like Tabitha's face either. It was pink like a doll's, with little piggy eyes, hardly human at all. She reminded me of a fat, spoiled pet—it was funny, because Disraeli had always seemed so much like a person.

I used to watch them. On one side of our rumpus room there was a long, narrow window, high up in the wall, to let in light, and if I climbed on a chair I could see right into the Hamiltons' back garden. I often stood there after school, watching Tabitha crawling around the grass with Disraeli beside her, and whenever she went anywhere near the railings of the swimming pool, he'd nudge her back, like a careful shepherd.

Sometimes I'd find Si watching there. He wasn't really so interested in Tabitha and Disraeli, but he was a spy by nature; he loved peering into people's private places. He was mad about the Hamiltons' pool, and he said the flat, level part of the yard would make a great place for a cricket pitch.

"Wish we lived there," he sighed. "It's wasted on a baby."

I thought of the window as my private spy hole, not his. "Get off," I said. He shoved me, and I pushed him back.

"It's a free world!" he shouted. "I was here first."

"It's mine!"

"Boys!" my mother called, and we scuttled away fast; she'd be mad if she caught us climbing on the furniture.

The Hamiltons began to have a problem with Tabitha at night, because she didn't like to sleep.

"She puts her down at six thirty," my mother told my father, "and then the kid screams for five hours straight. Why doesn't she just put her to bed a bit later?"

"Perhaps they want some peace and quiet," suggested my father.

"Well, they're not getting it, are they?"

Sometimes, just when Tabitha dropped off to sleep, Disraeli would begin his howling, and she'd wake up again and cry some more. Then Mr. Hamilton would poke his head out the window and shout, "Shut up!" in a hateful voice that made me want to kill him; and then Disraeli would be quiet, though Tabitha wouldn't.

One night at the beginning of autumn a storm came up, with lightning and thunder. Disraeli hated thunder; he howled and howled on a long, quivering note like a wolf lost in the snow. Mr. Hamilton shouted and shouted, but it wasn't any use at all. Then I heard their back door bang, and I thought joyfully, He's going to take him inside. But that didn't happen—instead there was a dull thump and a sharp yelp, and then silence. I can't tell you how I felt, hearing that yelp and remembering all over again how kindly the Hamiltons had once treated Disraeli, as if he'd been their child. It was all Tabitha's fault—if only she hadn't come along, with her fat, roly-poly body and her mean little piggy eyes. It was *her* fault, and I wished she'd vanish. . . . I wished she'd die in the night, like those babies you read about in the papers. I hated her.

The next afternoon I slipped out early from school. It was easy enough; we were having sport. I knew my mother wouldn't be home yet; she'd had a three o'clock appointment at the dentist. I'd still have to be quick though, because of Si—he got out of school at three thirty.

It was very quiet: that special kind of quietness you have

when all the kids are still at school. Mrs. Hamilton was asleep, I knew; she always slept in the afternoon. She felt Tabitha was safe enough, with Disraeli to guard her.

I crept through the back fence into the Hamiltons' yard. It was bright and warm and sunny after the storm, and there she was, little piggy eyes, out in the garden on her rug, with Disraeli nestling up beside her. I took those pudgy little hands of hers and walked her across the lawn, the way I'd seen Mrs. Hamilton do. Disraeli came up to me when he saw we were near the pool fence—he seemed suspicious, and for a moment I thought he was going to bark. "Good dog," I whispered. "Remember me? Good dog. Be quiet."

The funny thing was that afterward, when I was standing there, grasping Disraeli firmly by the collar, holding him back, and watching the blue sky glittering from the surface of the pool, I began to worry—not about what I'd done or Mrs. Hamilton coming out the back door and spotting me— but about this history project we had to do for school; it was due in on Friday, and I hadn't even started it.

That evening my mother came rushing into the kitchen. "Tabitha's drowned!" she cried. "She crawled through the fence somehow and fell into the pool and drowned. They found her floating, about five o'clock. The dog didn't bark or warn them—they've had him destroyed—" She put a hand to her mouth and burst into tears.

I couldn't take it in. They'd killed Disraeli!

"It's— it's like murder!" I shouted, and almost choked on the word.

"David!" my mother cried. "The Hamiltons have lost their child, and you go on about—"

"It wasn't Disraeli's fault Tabitha fell in the pool!" I burst out. "He didn't have anything to do with it."

My mother didn't reply. She was crying again.

"David was in there, Mum," Si said suddenly. "He knows."

"What?" She looked up, puffy with tears. "David, did you see—"

"I was *not* there," I said, kicking Si sharply on the ankle. "Si's always making up stories—he's raving. I haven't been in the Hamiltons' place for months."

Si punched me on the chest and I pulled him down on the floor and we scuffled and rolled about. He'd been spying out the window again: He'd seen me. When I was with Tabitha? Or just later, when I was on my own, coming back through the fence? It didn't matter, I thought, because he *did* tell stories—so many that no one believed a word he said. "You shut up!" I hissed.

My mother wasn't really listening to us. She whimpered, "Oh, God," and sank her head down on the table, and I knew her thoughts were far from us, fixed on little silent Tabitha, white and still, way down on the blue-green tiles.

Nobody knew. But I did. And so on certain nights I wake and hear the sound in the pool next door: that slow, even splashing, up and down and up and down—and once I got out of bed and ran into the Hamiltons' garden. I stood on the edge of the pool, but I saw nothing, even though the splashing was still going on in my ears, and there was a cold like ice rising up from the brown sludge and the rotting leaves. I wanted to shout, "Go home, Disraeli, go home!"

But where is home? And someone would have heard, and they might have guessed about me. So now, on those nights when I hear Disraeli swimming up and down, up and down, searching for Tabitha down beneath the water, I just lie.

15 Globe Street, Tarella

When I first saw Clightie Willis I went cold all over—to the tips of my fingers and toes and the tingling roots of my hair—and yet the word that came into my mind was "flame," which is silly because, as I said, it was cold I felt, not warmth at all.

I fell in love at first sight.

You hear people say that's a myth, an illusion, it doesn't happen—but they're wrong. Seeing her in the school corridor that first day, I felt I'd known her forever, and I'd learned from my mother's library books that this was a certain sign of love. Oh, I know those books are full of clichés, but clichés are true in a way, otherwise they wouldn't be clichés. I was fated to meet Clightie Willis: I was born for that moment, it was fate that made Mrs. Lander send me to the Headmaster's office that morning with a note. She'd never picked me to deliver a message before; I don't think she thought I could afford the time out of class.

I knocked on the Headmaster's door.

"Come in," he boomed. He was stacking a pile of papers in a drawer; Clightie's admission form was right on top, and in that split second before the papers slid out of sight I saw, printed on the form under PREVIOUS ADDRESS, the words: *15 Globe Street, Tarella*.

15 Globe Street, Tarella! I repeated it over and over as I walked home through the streets, and I repeated Clightie's name, and I saw her face exactly in my mind, just as though she was walking beside me.

She was utterly beautiful. I'd never thought much about what makes a girl beautiful—I'd never thought much about girls at all—but I knew that if I'd ever begun to make a picture in my head of a beautiful girl, she would have had a face like Clightie's: fair and broad, with high, flat cheekbones and long, slightly slanted gold-brown eyes. And her hair—that was the most marvelous thing of all. It was a rich, corn color done up in thick braids over the top of her head, like a crown.

The first thing I did when I reached home was to go to the bookcase in the living room and take out my dad's old atlas of Australia. I wanted to look up Tarella, and although there was no one in the house at the time, I felt it wasn't private enough there in the living room. I wanted to be by myself, really alone, so I went into my room and closed the door, to find Tarella in secret.

It was a little place down south, a tiny pinprick in miles of empty coast, its name printed so small that if you hadn't known the word to start with, you'd never have been able to make it out. A seaside town, I thought, and straightaway I could imagine it completely—I could *see* it: the clean, sandy streets and the neat white weatherboard cottages, the curve of pearly wet beach with the sea gulls walking gravely on their reflections.

15 Globe Street, Tarella! The address enchanted me; the sound of the words: the round fullness of Globe, the

airy lightness of Tarella—it was perfect to me, even dear. It fitted *her*, somehow.

And yet that was silly, I suppose, for Clightie didn't live there anymore. I didn't think of the silliness then; it was as if, on seeing Clightie, I'd entered straightaway another world, one where logic and reason didn't operate anymore. I spent a long time in my room that afternoon, thinking about Tarella, imagining the house Clightie had grown up in, all the rooms—they had polished wooden floors, I knew that, with tiny grains of sand caught between the cracks of the floorboards, and pale curtains blowing in and out of the windows, softly, with the breeze from the sea.

That night at dinner I couldn't eat anything. I wasn't hungry; I wanted to get back to my room and think some more about Clightie, about what I'd do and say, in the classes we shared, so that she'd get to notice me. I had to make a good impression. Eating wasn't important.

Straightaway my mother noticed my lack of appetite.

"I hope you're not getting that influenza that's going around," she said, "I've heard it *hangs on*." She turned to my father. "I *knew* I should have taken him to the doctor to get those shots. I'm sorry I didn't do it now; I can't afford to take time off work to look after *him*." The whiney note in her voice infuriated me. She was always being sorry for things she'd forgotten to do.

"He looks okay to me," said my father. "Probably been stuffing himself with chips and junk on the way home from school."

My mother whined afresh. She hated the local hamburger joint; she thought it was unhygienic. "Chris," she began, "have you been—"

My father cut her short. "Oh, leave the boy alone, Annie." He paused, and darted a short, sidelong glance in my direction. I saw his thick lips twitch; some joke was surfacing. "Perhaps he's fallen in love." He gave a low, grating chuckle that sounded like the Insinkerator going into action, chewing up garbage.

I hated him. I wished he'd fall down dead with a heart attack. Then I'd be bereaved, fatherless. Clightie would feel sorry for me.

She wasn't in any of my classes; I found that out over the next few days. Most of her subjects were different from mine: She did typing and home economics and media, and for those we shared, like English and math, she was in another group. Our names were at opposite ends of the alphabet: Adamson and Willis. So I didn't have the kind of easy chances you get to impress a girl if you're in the same class, like giving smart answers to the teacher or reading out your best essay in class, depending on the type of girl. Clightie, I knew, was the second sort.

That left lunch hours and recess, the chance of getting into conversation with her in the playground, casually, so it didn't look as if I was on the make. I had a kind of horror of her thinking that.

It would have been easy enough if she'd been on her own, or if she'd made friends with the girls I knew, but for some reason she'd palled up with Ellen Toomey and Debbie Forsythe. They were the loudest girls in school, a couple of real hormone cases, if you believed the rumors that went around. They were the type who thought if you even looked at a girl you fancied her, only they didn't put it like that—they said you "had the hots." I knew that's what they'd say if I went up and tried to speak to Clightie while she was with them; they'd stare and giggle while I spoke, and when I turned away, they'd double up with laughter—"He's got the hots for you, Clightie."

I couldn't face that; I'd have to catch her outside school, find out where she lived. It was useless looking in the telephone book; her family was new in town. I'd rung up directory inquiries, disguising my voice a bit, but they didn't have a new number for anyone called Willis. I soon found, waiting by the school gate, that she walked home with Debbie and Ellen, but I knew that if I tried to follow, those two would have spotted me at once; they were always on the lookout for that kind of thing. Already, after only a few days, I had this uncomfortable feeling that they *knew*. Ellen had seen me once in the playground, gazing over in their direction, and she'd given a little smile. I'd turned away quickly, so I didn't see if she'd nudged Clightie, but she might have. The idea tormented me for days afterward; I wished I hadn't turned away so fast. It was a dead give-away.

I couldn't understand why Clightie had taken up with Debbie and Ellen. They were the wrong sort of friends for her: They didn't fit her at all. She wasn't like them, I knew that, even though she'd taken to wearing her uniform in the way they did, hiked up so short you could see her knickers when she bent over, and the waist pulled in really tight so that the chest looked bigger. I figured *they* must have taken up with her, right on that first day, before she knew what they were like, and before she'd had time to get to know any of the other girls. And then, being a gentle kind of person, I suppose she didn't know how to get rid of them.

I'd had an experience like that when I first came to school and Kenny Larkin had started tagging around with me.

Kenny was the school dag, a tall, clumsy, white-faced boy.
Everyone called him "unco Kenny" because of his habit
of falling about, tripping over chair legs and bashing himself
on the sharp corners of desks and filing cabinets. He was
a disaster at gym: He could never get over the vaulting
horse or climb the ropes, and when we did aerobics, he
always had his left arm up in the air when everyone else
was using their right. He clowned about it, and this made
it worse somehow. No one ever laughed: He was too pathetic, and it's funny how, instead of feeling sorry for pathetic people, you shrink away as if they've got something
catching.

So when he tried to make friends with me, I gave him
the push, straight off—it doesn't do you any good to get
caught up with a loser. People start thinking you're one as
well.

I began hanging around the shopping center on Saturday
mornings, hoping I'd catch a glimpse of Clightie. And I
walked around the parks on Sunday because I knew that
would be the best thing: if I could somehow catch her really
alone, sitting on the grass by herself, thinking about Tarella, perhaps, and how she missed the place. Then it would
be okay, quite natural just to sit down and get into a conversation, about school and things like that; it wouldn't
look as if I was on the make. But I only ever saw her once,
and then she was with Ellen Toomey, outside Rosie's Rec-
ord Shoppe. I saw them going in, and I hung around outside
the newsagent opposite, hoping that when they came out,
they'd separate and each go home alone. But they came
out together and began to cross the road, and I slipped
quickly inside the newsagent and pretended to be browsing

through the car magazines. I don't think they noticed me—but you can never be sure.

I gave up a lot of things that term—the debating society, basketball, and Saturday Italian classes. I'd had this crazy idea about going to Rome when I finished school, getting a job, living in a little room high up above the streets, walking around those great big squares lined with palaces, where the pigeons fly up in a cloud at your feet. The idea seemed childish after I met Clightie, like a kid daydreaming about being an astronaut. Anyway, I gave up Italian; I needed those Saturday mornings now. I didn't want to be around other kids, either. When I was with them, I felt anxious to get away, as if time was wasting; their talk about football and parties and other girls drove me frantic. When I wasn't prowling the streets of the suburb, hoping to catch a glimpse of Clightie, I stayed in my room. If anyone had told me, a few months back, that I'd be living this kind of life, I wouldn't have believed them. It would have sounded like prison.

But I was happy in a way: Every evening, before going to sleep, I'd take out the old atlas of Australia from under my mattress, open it at page 43, and look at Tarella. Sometimes I even kissed it, like a photograph. Stupid, that was.

Now and again, as I lay in bed a night, a disturbing thought would come to me, like an echo from the old, ordinary world. I kept pushing the idea back, but it would surface again, sometimes waking me sharply in the middle of the night, like the nag of a tooth that is just about to begin aching. It was this: Surely if Clightie liked me, or even felt she *might* like me, then she'd try and talk to me herself, or at least give me the chance to talk to her. She'd get rid of Debbie and Ellen somehow, just for one afternoon—it wouldn't have been so difficult; she could have told them she had a dentist's appointment or something. Then she could walk home from school by herself, so that if I wanted to, I could catch her up. That's the kind of thing girls did when they liked someone. Barbara Pritchard, Phil Darby's girlfriend, had changed subjects last year just so she could get into his class and he'd notice her. I'd have tried to do this myself, but it was too near the end of the year. When someone liked you, they gave you a chance. And if Clightie wasn't doing this with me, then it meant . . .

But there were special considerations, I told myself. Clightie was shy; she must have been, otherwise she'd have made other friends among the girls. And Debbie and Ellen *were* possessive. Perhaps it really was impossible to get away from them, even for a moment, once they'd got their hooks well in. And she certainly wouldn't want to come up and speak to me in the playground with them about. They'd have given her a bad time; they'd say she had the hots for me: She probably hated the thought of their mockery as much as I did.

Time was passing; the holidays were getting nearer. At least in term time, although I couldn't speak to Clightie, I could catch glimpses of her at school. In December there wouldn't even be that. We were going away on holidays; probably she was too. And then it struck me: *Of course*—she'd go to Tarella; they'd have relatives there. And—*we* could go to Tarella; my parents were looking for a quiet spot to spend the holidays. My father wanted to do some fishing away from the crowds. And Clightie would never suspect I'd followed her. She had no idea I knew the place she'd come from; she'd think it was coincidence. . . . She might even think it was *fate*.

So when my parents began talking about where we'd go for the holidays, I broke in swiftly. "Let's go to Tarella," I said.

"Tarella?" queried my mother. "Where's that?"

"A little place down the coast, miles from anywhere. You said you wanted somewhere quiet."

"Fishing okay?" my father asked.

"Sure—there's tailor, luderick, whiting, salmon, and bream." I'd looked up Tarella in the local library and found it at last in a book called *Our Glorious Coastline*. "A small port and fishing resort," that's all it said, besides the list of fish.

"Where'd you hear about this place?"

"One of the kids at school went there last Christmas. He said it was great—really peaceful."

"I didn't think you kids went in for peace."

I shrugged. "He's that kind of kid. Quiet."

"What's his name?" pried my mother.

"Kenny Larkin," I replied. The name just popped into my head. It was safe enough; she didn't know him.

"Tarella, eh? I'll think about it," said my father. "Ask around a bit. There's a bloke at the office whose brother's in the travel business. . . ."

He was hooked, I could see.

The very next day I saw Clightie in the supermarket. She wasn't with Debbie and Ellen, but she wasn't alone, either. There was a stout, middle-aged woman with her, wheeling a laden trolley, and as I caught sight of them, Clightie took down a can of dog food from the shelves and dumped it on top of the groceries.

"Careful, Clightie," shrilled the woman, "there's eggs in there."

Clightie didn't notice me. "I'll go and get the cheese then, Mum," she said, and raced off toward the deli counter.

I glanced at Clightie's mother. She didn't fit: She wasn't at all what I'd expected. I'd imagined someone cool and tall and fair, perhaps with Clightie's plaited hairstyle, only in a dignified silver gray. This woman wasn't dignified at all. She was short and red faced; her hair was curly and a nondescript brown shade; she wore a print frock and a saggy pink cardigan. I'd seen her about the shopping center lots of times when I'd been out looking for Clightie. I'd follow *her*, I decided—not today, not with Clightie, but next time I saw her on her own.

I didn't have long to wait. She was there in Union Road the very next Monday afternoon, standing at the bus stop outside Woolworths. I stood there too, and when the bus came, I climbed on board right behind her. She was slow with her change, and because I had a school pass, the driver waved me on. I sat near the front of the bus, thinking she'd sit behind where there were empty double seats, but she squeezed in beside me, dumping her bulging string bags on the floor near my feet.

"Mind your toes, love," she said, and there was something in the tone of her voice, something coarse and unlovely, that reminded me of the voices of Debbie Forsythe and Ellen Toomey.

"Phew!" She sighed gustily, mopping at her face with a big checked handkerchief. "Hot enough for you? Summer's coming in with a vengeance."

I nodded, edging away into the corner of the seat. She smelled of sweat and peppermint.

" 'Spose you're looking forward to the school holidays. Going away?"

"Yes."

"Lucky old you. We're not going anywhere this summer. We've just moved—well, you'd know about that—Clightie being new and all."

I gazed at her in shock: She *knew* about me! They must have seen me after all, Debbie and Ellen—and Clightie. They'd been laughing about me; they'd told her mum. And—they weren't going to Tarella after all!

Mrs. Willis peered at me. "Don't you know Clightie then? Thought you would—you go to the same school, don't you? I can tell by the uniform."

So that was it! Weak with relief, I smiled. "I've seen her about," I said. "I'm in her year."

"Are you? I'd have thought you were younger, about fourteen or so."

"I'm sixteen."

"Small for your age. Still, they say good things come in small parcels, don't they?" She chuckled. "Sorry, I know you kids like to look as old as possible; it's a wicked shame, really." She shook her head. "I've been on to Clightie about her hair."

"Her hair?"

"Those plaits she wears, that old-fashioned style; she looks like my aunt Mabel. I've been trying to get her to go down to Irene's and get it cut properly, get a bit of a curl—perms are no problem these days."

"Oh *don't*," I blurted, forgetting myself. "I think her hair looks marvelous like that."

She gave a short bark of laughter. "Marvelous, eh? You're a funny one, and no mistake. Like plaits, do you?"

"I mean—it's much better than those punk cuts and stuff like that."

"Punk cuts? Oh, you mean Deb and Ellie. Aren't they a sight? Still, it's all the rage these days. Those plaits, they're a real nuisance—takes her half an hour to do them up in the mornings. Then she's late for school, hasn't time to make her bed or tidy up her room. I spend half the day picking up after her. Sometimes I think she does it to spite me—keeps her hair long, I mean, just because she knows I don't like it. She's a real little madam sometimes, I can tell you."

I didn't answer.

"Live around here, do you?"

"Um, no—my aunt does. I'm visiting my aunt."

"Visiting your aunt!" She grinned. "Well, you are an old-fashioned boy. You don't catch many kids these days out visiting their relatives."

I didn't know what to say. Mrs. Willis bent down and began gathering up her bags. "Well, here's my stop coming up." Unsteadily she rose to her feet. "Love you and leave you."

I got out at the next stop; it was only a few yards down the road. In the distance I could see Mrs. Willis's lumpy figure trudging along slowly; I kept a good way off. I didn't think, laden down as she was, that she'd turn around and spot me, but you could never be sure. She crossed the road and went through the gateway of a small block of flats. I waited a few minutes, till I could be sure she was safely inside; then I hurried along the road. There was a narrow fenced laneway opposite, and I stood in there, concealed by the high fences and the cars parked in the roadway.

I stared across at the flats. They were drab and ugly, a glaring yellow brick with black drainpipes crawling down the side. There were flats like that all over our suburb—Ashwood was an ugly place altogether. I hated it; I'd hated it for a long time. I felt I didn't fit there, just as Clightie didn't. I wanted us to live somewhere that was clean and beautiful, like Tarella. Poor Clightie, how she must miss that place, the sandy roads and the white cottages and the clean sweep of the sea.

As I crouched there, a boy came walking along the footpath outside the flats. He paused by the gate and stared up at the windows. I recognized that thin, lanky form, the white face, the clumsiness of his movements. It was Kenny Larkin. Kenny Larkin, staring up at Clightie's windows! Even from that distance I could see the expression on his face: the hot, anxious eyes, the foolish, gape-mouthed yearning.

He stood there, in full view of everyone, gawking. He was *mad*—she'd *see* him, she'd laugh, she'd mash him to pieces with her rage and scorn. As if a dag like unco Kenny, a clown, a loser, could ever stand a chance with a girl like Clightie Willis! She wouldn't even look at him, and she'd hate him for looking at her, for even thinking of her. It made me sick too; it made me feel like throwing up on the footpath, the idea of Kenny Larkin lying in bed at night, thinking of Clightie.

The door of the flats banged: Debbie Forsythe and Ellen Toomey came rushing out, Clightie a little way behind them. The glint of her hair in the sunlight was all I saw before I turned and ran. Behind me, I heard Debbie and Ellen break into great whooping roars of laughter—their thick, raucous voices flapped and flurried in my ears: "Kenny's got the ho-ots, Kenny's got the ho-ots!"

* * *

Tarella was just as I'd known it would be. Everything was there: the clean sweep of beach, the neat white weatherboard cottages, the sandy streets. Every day my father set out for his fishing places on the rocks or riverbank; my mother was content to sit out on the sunny porch of our cottage, reading her library books and knitting against the winter. I was free to go where I pleased, and I wandered about the town, looking at the places Clightie must have known by heart: the single street of shops, the school set up on the grassy rise above the sea, the showground down behind the railway line, the dusty Botanical Gardens.

I walked along Globe Street every day, pausing to gaze at number 15, taking in the white curtains at the windows, the glimpse of yellow polished floors through the half-open front door, the baskets of maidenhair fern swinging from the roof of the verandah. It was marvelous to be able to gaze as long as I pleased, with no one around to catch me out, no Debbie Forsythe or Ellen Toomey. And it was even nice in a way that Clightie wasn't here—I didn't have to worry about what I'd say to her and how I'd act, and what she'd think of me.

It's funny—I loved her; I should have been sorry she was stuck back in grimy Ashwood with Mrs. Willis nagging on about her hair, but I wasn't. I was glad she hadn't gone away, off to places like Sydney or the Gold Coast where she might have met strangers, where something might have happened to her that I didn't know about. She was safe back there. Kenny Larkin was no threat: I knew he'd hang about. The laughter wouldn't put him off; he was used to people laughing at him—I knew he wouldn't get anywhere.

* * *

But after a week or so, I began to get bored with wandering in Clightie's old places; I was impatient for something more. I wanted to talk to someone who'd known Clightie; I wanted to say her name aloud to someone. I'd seen a few kids my age in town, but kids were too sharp. I felt they'd guess why I asked about her.

I decided on old Mr. Bruner, who ran the store where we bought our newspapers and milk.

"I go to school with a girl who grew up in this place," I remarked casually as I picked up the *Herald* from the counter.

"Do you now?" He wasn't all that interested.

"Clightie Willis," I informed him.

"Clightie who?"

"Willis."

He scratched his head, peering at me blearily through his spectacles. It was puzzling; he didn't seem to remember her.

"They lived at 15 Globe Street," I said. "You know, that place with the maidenhair ferns along the verandah."

"Minnie Peters's place."

"Minnie Peters?" He must have got it wrong. "This girl," I went on, "Clightie Willis—she came from 15 Globe Street."

He shook his head.

"She did," I burst out. "I know, I saw the address on— I mean, she told me."

"Okay, son, keep your shirt on. I wasn't arguing with you. Just said it was Minnie Peters's place, and it is. I should know; I went to school with Minnie Peters—years ago, that was, we're both getting on now. She's lived in that house all her life; her dad bought it just after the War.

First World War that was—the Great War, we called it. We thought—"

"But Clightie said—"

"Hold on, I'm coming to that. A few months back, Minnie went off to England to visit her daughter, and she rented the place out for a bit, to those— What did you say the name was?"

"Willis."

"Yeah—to the Willises. They didn't stay long, not more than a few weeks. There isn't much work around here—don't know why they came, really."

"You mean—Clightie didn't live here when she was little? She didn't go to that school up on the hill, the one with the water tank in the playground?" (I'd drunk from the enamel cup, fixed to the tank stand with a length of chain.)

Mr. Bruner looked at me queerly. "I don't know what school she went to, son. Like I said, she was only here for a bit, a month at most."

I couldn't take it in. Ever since I'd seen that address in the Headmaster's office, I'd been dreaming about this place, imagining Clightie here as a little girl, Clightie growing up: It had been part of her, it had fitted exactly. Tarella *was* Clightie: It was almost everything I knew of her. Now it was gone, taken away from me, and for an instant, sickeningly, I couldn't remember her face.

"Something the matter, son?"

"No, no." I held out my hand as he counted out change.

"I recall her now," he said slowly. "Tall girl, wasn't she? Blonde? Hair done up in a plait, old-fashioned?"

"Yes."

"Quite a looker!" He winked.

Clutching my *Herald*, dazed, I wandered out the door.

* * *

"Let's go this way," said my mother. It was our last day. Every evening, when Dad went down to the rocks, my mother and I took a walk: Mostly we strolled along the beach or through the Botanical Gardens. This evening, as luck would have it, she turned up Globe Street. "Let's go this way."

We walked silently along the sandy road. The sun was setting, the white walls of the cottages flushed pink, geraniums glowed like lanterns behind the fences. As we approached number 15, I closed my eyes; I felt I didn't want to look at the house again.

"Pretty little cottages, aren't they?" I heard my mother say. "It's really a lovely spot. It was very clever of you to discover it, Chris."

"Someone told me," I muttered.

And then, as we came near the end of the street, I did turn around for one last look. After all, Clightie *had* lived there for a few weeks, and it was just possible she'd fallen in love with it, that even in so short a time the house and Tarella had become a part of her. I gazed down the street . . . and there, turning in at the gate of number 15, I saw two figures: a tall girl with plaited hair and a lanky, pale-faced boy whose clumsy gait was quite unmistakable. Kenny Larkin. I closed my eyes again, and when I opened them the pair had vanished, gone in through the front door.

"Something wrong?" asked my mother.

"Nothing," I snapped. "Let's go home. It'll be getting dark soon."

It couldn't have been them, I thought, lying on my bed with the door closed against my parents' voices: It must have been some kind of hallucination. The Willises hadn't been going away—Mrs. Willis had said so, and even if they'd changed their minds, cramped up in the stifling flat, they certainly wouldn't bring Kenny Larkin; the very idea was ridiculous.

It must have been a mistake. I'd seen someone else—Mrs. Peters's granddaughter, perhaps. She could have copied Clightie's hairstyle. And Kenny? The granddaughter might have a friend who looked like him—no, that was impossible, too much of a coincidence. The questions went around and around in my head until I felt sick, and even mad. I wished now I'd kept my eyes open; then I would have seen them coming along the street toward me. I could have been sure.

I could ask Mum. She'd have seen them: She always noticed people, particularly kids of my age. I'd ask her; she'd think it odd, but I didn't care: I had to be sure.

She was washing dishes in the kitchen, and Dad, thank heavens, had turned in for an early night.

"Mum," I began. She turned around, smiling at me, glad I'd come in for a chat.

"Yes?"

"When we went out for our walk this evening—"

"Yes?"

"When we were going up Globe Street—"

"Globe Street? Where's that?"

"Oh, *you* know—that street with the white cottages. There's one with maidenhair ferns on the verandah, and you stopped and said it was pretty."

"Well, it *is* pretty around here. I'm so glad we—"

"Just *think*! Just there, as we walked on, did you see two people coming down the street, a tall girl with plaited hair, and a thin boy, sort of pale—a pale boy?"

She screwed up her eyes. "A girl with plaits? You don't

see many girls with their hair in plaits these days. A pity, really."

"Yes, I *know*. But did you see one just there, in Globe Street, coming toward us?"

"I don't remember. I wasn't really—"

"Try!" I felt like shaking her. "Did you?"

"I can't say. I don't think so, really. It seemed pretty quiet, getting on for teatime. No, I don't think—"

I turned away.

"But of course, I can't be sure. They could have been on the other footpath; I mightn't have noticed them. I was looking at the houses. Why? Is it someone you know? Someone you met in the town?"

"No, I—"

She peered at me. "You don't look well, Chris, kind of peaked, and on your holiday! Are you all right? You've spent practically the whole of the last two days in your room. Is anything the matter?"

"I'm okay. I had a few books to read for school."

She pursed her lips. "I don't believe in teachers giving work over the holidays," she pronounced. "There's enough of it in term time."

I went back to my room and switched out the light. I waited half an hour, till I could be sure she'd think I was asleep and wouldn't come tapping at my door; then I climbed out of the window and turned up the street toward Mr. Bruner's store. He kept late hours sometimes; he'd be there, and I could ask him if the Willises had come back to town in the last few days. They couldn't have been there when I spoke to him, or he'd have mentioned they were back.

But the shop was closed, and no one came when I knocked at the door; he must have been out.

I hurried round to Globe Street and crept through the gate. The buffalo grass pricked my bare feet, and the sharp pebbles on the side path dug in hard as I sneaked around the outside of the house like a thief, spying in the windows. There was a light on at the back, and through a gap in the curtains I saw an old lady sitting in front of the television, a cat curled around in her lap. Mrs. Peters. There was no one else in the room. The other windows were curtained and dark; I didn't know if anyone was in there or not.

But suddenly it didn't matter, for I knew now what I'd seen. A ghost. It was quite clear to me: Something had happened to Clightie, some accident or horrible illness, and she'd died. And her ghost had come back to 15 Globe Street, Tarella, because she knew I'd be passing there, and that I loved her. As for Kenny—I didn't know, I couldn't be bothered thinking about him.

The very moment we got home, Mum wanted me to go down to the supermarket for her.

"I've got to go somewhere," I said.

"Where? Where have you got to go?" The long drive back had made her cranky. "There's nowhere you have to go, Christopher, except round to the market to get me these things, and be quick about it!"

I went—it wouldn't take long anyway. But all the way there I was terrified I'd meet someone, some kid from school who'd yell out, "Hey, guess what? Clightie Willis is dead. . . ." I couldn't bear that; I couldn't stand for someone else to tell me. I had to find out for myself, go around to the flat, knock on the door, wait until Mrs. Willis answered, her eyes red and swollen with weeping.

But the only kid I saw down at the supermarket was

Clightie herself, just coming through the sliding doors, gaily swinging one of her mother's string bags. I went right up to her; I wasn't nervous anymore.

"I've been to Tarella," I said boldly.

"Tarella?" She gave a kind of sneer and tossed her head. "That dump! Why'd you go there?"

"I went on holidays, and I saw you there."

"Saw me? How could you? I was here—been here all the time. Last place I'd go would be Tarella, anyway; it bores me stiff."

"I *saw* you," I repeated. "Outside your house—15 Globe Street. You were going in the gate."

She frowned, and I laughed weakly. "I thought you were a ghost, Clightie. I thought you'd *died*!" My voice rose to a kind of shout, and she drew back a little.

"Died?" She sounded frightened. "How could I be dead when I'm here?"

I faltered. "I don't know. I—"

She shifted the string bag to her other hand. Through its meshes I could see what the Willises would have for tea: a tin of ham, tomatoes, white sliced bread.

"It's funny you should say that, though," she said, a puzzled expression in her eyes. "I mean, about being dead."

"Why?" I asked. "Why is it funny?"

"Well—because someone *did* die. Kenny Larkin. He fell under a bus, right near our place. I didn't see it, because I was out with Ellie and Deb, but poor Mum did." She lowered her voice. "It was *awful*—Mum chucked up on the footpath, right in front of everyone; it was the shock, you know, seeing something horrible like that. The wheel went right over his head."

There was a silence, then Clightie sighed gustily. "Wouldn't you just *know* an unco kid like Kenny Larkin would fall under a bus someday? He was made for it; he had two left feet, that guy." She wagged her head. Her voice was soft now, confidential, but in it I caught the echo of that coarse, unlovely tone she shared with Ellen and Debbie and her mother. "Kenny was always hanging around our place, you know. Sniffing about, like a dog." Clightie sniffed too, contemptuously. "Randy—that was his trouble; that's what Deb and Ellie said."

I went cold all over just like that first day: my fingertips and toes, the roots of my hair. Something burned out in me. I turned and ran.

That night I dreamed of Kenny Larkin.

Scared Stiff

I'm scared stiff. Not just now, this minute, but every minute of my life, ever since I was a baby. I don't remember what scared me when I was little, but there would have been *something*. Probably the rattle: I don't like rattles. I don't like the noise they make, hollow and creepy, like *bones*, like loose teeth chattering inside a skull.

This morning's bad, really bad: I think I had that dream about the weather house again, and it scared me stiff, so I woke at dawn, before the birds were up. I was glad they weren't up; I'm frightened of that special way they chatter in the early mornings, really loud and urgent, as if they're trying to tell me something, warn me . . .

That weather house: of all the things I'm scared of in this house—the mirror in my mother's bedroom with the little forked crack at the corner; the cold, snakey chain that holds the bath plug in place; the pattern of squares on the living-room carpet; so many things—it's the weather house that scares me most. I don't know why—it's just a little cottage with a pointed roof, an open door with a window on each side, and two stiff wooden figures, a lady and a man: Mr. Rain, in a dark suit with a furled umbrella at his side, and Mrs. Sun, with her blue skirt and yellow blouse and the basket hanging on her arm. I try not to look at it when I go into the kitchen, but that's impossible. It's funny how when you're trying not to look at something, you simply can't help catching sight of it; whichever way you turn your head, there seems to be a corner of it sliding into your eye.

In the dream the weather house is big, like a real house, and the weather must be changing, because Mr. Rain, with his furled umbrella, is creeping back inside; the doorway is empty, and I'm standing there waiting for Mrs. Sun to come out. And all the time I'm terrified, scared stiff that when she does appear, something bad will happen to me.

There go the birds: They're really loud this morning. They're telling me something I can't quite figure out, even though I listen with all my might.

Thump! That's the newspaper landing on the front step. I'm scared stiff of that sound; I keep thinking it's not the newspaper at all, but a great big enormous footstep: someone coming for me. When I told Tracey Lyons this, she burst out laughing. "Must be a one-legged man," she giggled, and then she told all the kids that I was mental; she's not my friend anymore.

There's Mum in the kitchen now, making breakfast. She's sick of me, and you can't blame her; I'm scared of just about everything, and it makes life difficult for her. I'm terrified of trains: It started when I was little. I was afraid I'd fall down that big gap between the platform and the carriage, and I used to kick up a great noisy fuss, screaming and tugging at Mum's skirt, refusing to get on, so the train would pull out of the station and leave us behind. Now I'm too big to fall down that gap, but it makes no difference to me. I'm still scared of trains: I won't go anywhere unless it's on a bus route. She's fed up with me. I've got this feeling she's going to throw me out; she's just waiting till I'm sixteen, in two months' time, so I can leave school and get a job. Then she's going to say, "Margaret, I want you to move out." Just like that.

Where will I go? Some boardinghouse, I suppose—I'm scared stiff of boardinghouses. Tracey Lyons's big brother lived in one: It had dark old furniture and a hot plate, and weird people living in the rooms next door.

I'll get dressed and fetch the newspaper for Mum; she likes to read it while she's having breakfast.

Thank goodness the weather's all right. It's one of those soft, gray days, very still and calm. I'm scared stiff of wind, especially the north wind, the way it swoops and hurls itself about the sky, tugging at your hair and clothes as if it's going to lift you up and carry you away. I won't go out when it's windy; I don't go to school. The principal keeps ringing Mum up at work; it makes her really shitty. I think they're talking about sending me to a psychiatrist, but it won't work; I know it won't. I'm scared stiff of psychiatrists, scared of being locked up somewhere, like that place in *One Flew Over the Cuckoo's Nest*, where you've got to take pills and walk around all day in a nightie with strings at the back.

There, I've got the paper, and there's nothing terrible on the front page, no wars or earthquakes or stock-market crashes. But now I have to go into the kitchen, where the weather house is hanging. I wish I could close my eyes, but Mum won't have it; she says if she catches me walking around the house with my eyes closed again, she's going to stop my pocket money, and I need it to buy chocolates.

I wish I knew where my father was, or who he was, so I could look up his name in the telephone directory and find him. Mum never talks about him; she won't even tell me his name. He went away before I was born. I did see him once, years ago when I was really little—I was playing by myself in the backyard and this strange man came up the alley and stood at our gate. "Margaret!" he called, holding out his arms to me—and I ran across the yard, and he lifted me up and whirled me around in the air and then held me up close against him. I don't know how he knew my name, and you'd think I'd have been scared stiff, a stranger coming to the gate like that, grabbing me up in his arms, but I wasn't: I was happy. Then Mum came out and drove him away, screaming and screaming like she does when I won't get on the train.

I'm eating my cornflakes, but my hand is trembling, showering milk on the table. It's because, although I'm looking down at the plate, all the time I keep seeing the weather house in my mind: Mr. Rain is out, standing there by the door with his furled umbrella.

Is he? He might be, because it's such a gray, misty day— I've got to look, I've got to, something is forcing me.

No, I won't. I'll look at Mum instead.

She's reading the classifieds; she's looking for a boarding-house, the kind that takes in girls! In a moment she'll raise her head and say, "Margaret, I want you to move out next week. Take your things and go."

"Margaret—"

Oh, God, it's coming.

"Margaret, I want you to go round to Mr. Tilba's place and get me a dozen eggs."

It's all right! She's not going to chuck me out, not just yet. But— but I'm scared stiff of Mr. Tilba's place. I don't know why.

"Can't I get them at the store? It's quicker."

"No, you can't. I want free-range eggs, and I want them this morning, before you go to school. Mr. Tilba doesn't like people going round to his house in the evenings."

"But— but I'm scared of Mr. Tilba!"

She doesn't answer this. She just says, "Margaret, go now and get the eggs," and her eyes are full of threats.

I stumble to the sink with my empty plate; it falls from my hand and crashes on the draining board, though luckily it doesn't break. I look up, and there's the weather house, right in front of my eyes: the door, the windows, the sharp, pointed roof. It can't be going to rain after all, because Mrs. Sun is standing there.

Oh— no! Oh, no! I can't believe it. I'm wearing exactly the same clothes as Mrs. Sun: a blue skirt and yellow blouse. Even my hair is the same: shiny black, close to my head, parted in the middle.

"Margaret, will you stop dithering and *go*!"

"I can't, I can't—I'm wearing the same clothes as Mrs. Sun."

"What?"

"I'm wearing the same clothes as the lady in the weather house. Look: a blue skirt and a yellow blouse and— and black hair! I'll have to go and change. I'll have to change right away!"

"No, you *won't*. I've never heard such nonsense, even from you. There isn't time for you to change, anyway. I want those eggs here, in this kitchen, before I leave for work. So just take the money, and this basket, and *go*."

"Basket!"

"What's the matter *now*?"

"Mum— Mum, I can't take the basket."

"Why not, for God's sake?"

"Don't you see? Mrs. Sun's got a basket hanging over

her arm, and if I take it, then I'll be exactly like her, and something bad will happen to me!"

Mum grabs me by the hair and shoves me out the door. She slams it shut, and I hear the bolt shoot fast on the other side. She sticks her head out through the kitchen window and yells, "I'll let you in when you get back here with those eggs, and not a moment sooner!" The basket falls at my feet, and a two-dollar coin. I pick it up—the coin, that is.

"Margaret, pick up that basket this minute. I don't want those eggs broken."

"But, Mum—"

"Pick it up!"

I stoop and, shuddering all over, slide the dreadful thing over my arm. Something bad will happen *now*, I think, screwing my eyes shut—but it doesn't, I'm still here, still Margaret.

I hurry out the gate, I start running—in ten minutes, nine minutes, seven and a half, it will all be over; I'll be back home, safe. I won't go to school today: When Mum's left for work, I'll get into bed, stay there all day, and recover. I'm scared stiff of school anyway.

It's raining now, a soft rain, like mist—and here's Mr. Tilba's place. I don't know why it scares me. It's just an ordinary house with a door in the middle, a window on each side, and a pointed roof. It's like—*like the weather house!* It is. It's exactly like the weather house. I'd never noticed before, never—I just knew I was scared stiff of it, but I—

"Good morning, Margaret."

It's Mr. Tilba. Standing beside the open door, in his dark suit, with a furled umbrella, his black hair slicked down with oil glistening like new paint. Of course—it's raining, so he *had* to come outside and stand beside the door: because he's Mr. Rain. Mr. Tilba is Mr. Rain!

I won't—I won't go in. But I have to. I've got to get the eggs, or Mum won't let me in the house anymore. I'll close my eyes.

When I reach the door, I say, very fast, "I want a dozen eggs, please," and the sentence comes out in a kind of gabble. It's always like this when I talk; I'm so scared stiff, the words come out too fast, running into one another, so it sounds like I'm talking in another language, one that nobody can understand. Or else I'm frozen, and the words come out so slow that people walk away before I've finished speaking.

Mr. Tilba understands me all right. He takes my arm and leads me inside his house, his fingers hard and chilly through the thin stuff of my yellow blouse. The eggs are ready on the table, and he packs them carefully into the basket for me. "Your mother rang," he says softly. "She thought you mightn't get here, but you did, didn't you? I knew you'd come. I told her not to worry."

All at once the sun comes out: a brilliant beam shines through the kitchen window, scaring me stiff. "Ah, the sun." Mr. Tilba smiles. "Now I can have a little rest." He slides the basket back onto my arm and gives it a gentle pat. "Now you must go outside," he says firmly, "and stand beside the door."

"What?"

"Go and stand by the door." He leads me out of the kitchen and up the hall to the place by the open door. "Stand," he says.

I stand, in my blue skirt and yellow blouse, with my neat black hair parted in the middle, and the basket over my arm.

I stand because I can't do anything else. I can't *move*. I'm turning stiff all over, wooden and hard; my blue skirt is glistening like fresh paint. I try to touch it, but I can't; one arm is frozen to my side, and the other is frozen to the basket. Everything is going dark and silent: I can't see—

I can't hear—

I can't speak—

I can't—think—

I'm—

SCARED STIFF.

The Torment of Mr. Gully

In April 1958 it rained for seventeen days straight. Thick, solid rain, great silver sheets flapping and billowing over the flat gray suburbs of the west.

Occasionally the clouds thinned and drifted and the rain dwindled to a fine cobwebby mist, but this was never for long and mostly just before dawn, when people were sound asleep and couldn't see that the stars and the moon were still there after all.

When daylight came, the clouds were back again, layer on layer like inky wads of cotton wool, so that the light was a thick brown gloom and the people inside it walked with their heads bent and their ears filled with the sounds of rushing, roaring, swooping water.

Marsden High stood on a hill—that was its name, "the school on the hill"—a name repeated monotonously throughout the school song, which closed each morning assembly. It was a tall brick building three stories high, with long, Gothic windows and a pointed roof. You could see it for miles around, for the hill was the only one on the plain, and almost all the children who went there had a view of Marsden from the yards or windows of their homes.

It was a school for clever kids: the ones who did well in the sixth-class examinations, who had, as the teachers informed their disbelieving parents, "high I-Gews." It sounded a bit like a disease, but Marsden had many famous ex-students: scholars and lawyers and cricketers and lord mayors. They had other kinds of graduates as well: drunks and dropouts and jailbirds and housewives, but these were not remembered or held up as examples.

The kids came from all over the western suburbs, suburbs that, though scattered, were curiously similar, with their wide, dusty streets and shabby prefab houses, their poky little corner shops and vacant lots filled with high paspalum grass and drifting yellowed sheets of the *Cumberland Advertiser*. The kids got up early and traveled miles on lumbering old buses and crowded trains, dressed in the clumsy, dark-blue uniform that suggested gruel and barred windows and orphans left on the workhouse doorstep.

In those wet days of April, raincoats were no protection: The thick blue serge of tunics and trousers grew dense and heavy in the wet, the brims of the girls' velour hats filled up with water, turned down and poured waterfalls, shoes squeaked and squelched and pulped. No one brought spare clothes, for you weren't allowed to change: "Uniforms must be worn at all times." There was nowhere to dry off; fires weren't lit in the schoolroom grates until after the May holidays.

Not that it was cold—the rainy days were warm and clammy, steamy as the tropics. The windows fogged up and the rooms reeked of wet wool. Decades later, for those adults who had once been kids in 1D, that particular smell, musky and faintly peppery, would evoke images of wooden walls and rain falling out of the sky, and with these images would come a shamed, shrinking feeling, and a sense of wrong done.

Down at the bottom of the hill, far below the tall brick building with the Gothic windows, there was a cluster of flimsy wooden portable classrooms set down in a field of greasy yellow clay. This was where the First Years were housed, four classes of them, and 1D was in the smallest shack, way down near the back fence, so far away from everyone else that the class had a feeling they had been put there on purpose, out of the way.

It might have been so, for 1D had acquired something of a reputation. It had happened simply, as such things often do: In the first week of the term some of the girls had been rather noisy in Miss Smiley's French class. They'd had a reason of sorts: Stepping out of the train at Summer Hill station, they'd seen a man drop down dead on the platform. None of the girls had ever seen a person die before, and they hadn't been able to get certain details out of their minds before Miss Smiley breezed through the door with *Contes et Legends* under her arm. They'd muttered to each other all through the lesson, and Miss Smiley had remarked in the staff room later that she found 1D a very noisy bunch. This remark was passed about. 1D's teachers became sensitive to noise; if there was so much as a whisper, they'd say, "I've heard that you're a pretty noisy bunch." 1D felt this was unfair: They knew they were no noisier than the kids in 1B or 1C. They sensed injustice, and its sting made them more restless and talkative than they had been—and so the reputation stuck and, in a way, became justified.

On these wet, gloomy days the 1D girls stood in a row on the edge of the verandah, wringing the hems of their soaking tunics and emptying their shoes onto the glossy mud below. The boys, wet and muddy beyond caring, hurled themselves from the verandah and slid on the backs of their heels down the sticky slope toward the wire fence that surrounded the school grounds. They hit the wire and bounced back, showering great globs of yellow mud into the air. Their skins were blotched with it, like big freckles.

The long days of rain had made 1D wild. At first they'd been excited, wonder-struck, and then, as it went on unceasingly day after day, they became a little scared, even panicky. They remembered Sunday School lessons about the Flood, and summer evangelists prophesying Doomsday on the beaches of Cronulla and Sans Souci and Brighton-le-Sands.

But as the rain continued and there was no Flood, the panic subsided and simple hysteria took over. When the bell rang at five past nine, they hurtled inside the portable and crowded up to the windows: From there they had a good view of the steep, treacherous path the teachers must descend to reach the portables from the main building: small flights of concrete steps set into the hillside down which the rain cascaded in miniature waterfalls, slippery unsurfaced stretches in between.

Massed silently behind the steamy glass, 1D waited expectantly for the small raincoated figures to emerge from the covered way at the top of the hill. They waited for slipups and falls, a broken arm or leg; at the very least, indignity. But the teachers, as if aware of these expectations, trod with the delicacy and skill of tightrope walkers—no one came to grief except for little old Amy Austen, who dropped a pile of Ancient History essays in the middle of a waterfall, so that the sharp, old-fashioned comments in perfect copperplate writing were lost forever.

Some of the teachers didn't bother to come in the wet. They said they didn't want to risk their necks for the sake of 1D: an hour's history or mathematics wouldn't be missed down there. They stayed upstairs in the cozy fug of the staff room, browsing through *Picture Post* or doing the *Sydney Morning Herald* crossword.

Only Mr. Gully always came, tottering slowly down the slope, umbrella in one hand, old brown suitcase in the other. Even in fine weather he was slow enough getting down that hill, ancient as he was and hindered by the weight of his luggage. Mr. Gully taught science, and his subject, for the whole of that first term, was certain basic laws of physics, which he demonstrated with the aid of a set of glass force pumps. The pumps were carried in the old cardboard suitcase, its front and sides plastered with luggage labels so ancient and blurred that even the sharpest eyes in 1D couldn't make them out.

Mr. Gully's method of taking a lesson never varied: He walked stiffly, slowly, through the door and across the front of the room, deposited the suitcase on the teacher's table, stood back a little, and delivered his greeting to the class: "Good morning, young ladies and gentlemen." 1D never replied beyond a mumble and a few giggles; they were shocked and embarrassed by the queer formality of such a greeting. "Nuts," they whispered to each other, tapping their foreheads and rolling their eyes in the teacher's direction. Then Mr. Gully stepped up close to the table, pulled back the catches on the old case, and carefully drew out the glass force pumps, one by one.

Slowly, oh so slowly, he demonstrated how each pump worked, and what its working meant in terms of physics. But by the time he got to the crux of the matter—if there was a crux, and 1D felt sure there couldn't be—the class had long stopped listening. People were writing notes and passing them to each other across the room; they were reading library books and comics and the sports pages of the morning newspaper. They were twisted around in their desks playing boxes and noughts-and-crosses with their neighbors.

Mr. Gully didn't seem to notice their inattention: He went on demonstrating the principles illustrated by the force pumps just as if they'd all been listening, and when he'd finished, he turned his back to the class and began writing those principles up on the board in his perfectly upright, perfectly legible handwriting, which 1D (for no reason they could think of except that they loathed old Gully and his suitcase of pumps) always pretended they couldn't understand.

"Please, sir, is that an *f* or a *g*?" Jimmy Cooney would call out from his place at the back of the room, and then Martin Kingston, a few seats in front, would echo, "Please, sir, is that a *g* or an *f*?"

Patiently Mr. Gully would pause in his chalky labors and seek out the offending letter. He'd consider it for a long moment, his heavy old head tilted to one side, and then slowly, slowly, he'd moisten his finger with spit (*Ugh! Ugh! Ugh!* cried the girls), rub out the letter, and replace it with an even more perfectly printed one.

"Gee, thanks, sir," called Jimmy Cooney, and "Thank *you*, sir" echoed his mate, Martin Kingston.

They'd complain about his soft voice, too. At a nod or a wink from Jimmy or Glenys Styles, hands would shoot up all over the class.

"Please, sir, we can't hear."

Obligingly, Mr. Gully would raise his creaky old voice a

few decibels, reeling out the facts and figures that no one bothered to take down.

This very obligingness infuriated 1D. What kind of teacher behaved like that? If you told Sarky Davis, the math teacher, that you couldn't make out his figures on the board, he'd just tell you to get a pair of glasses or move up to the front. And if you complained that you couldn't hear what he was saying, he'd most likely bawl out, "Shut up and you will!" And it was quite in the cards he'd hand you a detention for giving cheek; if he was in a certain mood, you might even get the cane.

Most of the teachers, though not quite such hard cases as Sarky Davis, were fairly strict. They stood no nonsense, and they made that clear from the moment you arrived at the school on the hill. If you didn't shape up, you could ship out—out to the Tech or the Domestic Science college or those high schools down the line that took in every Tom, Dick, and Harry.

Old Gully was too soft. He wasn't a good teacher, 1D decided; otherwise, why did he listen to them when they complained? And they complained, they knew, only for fun. Old Amy was just as ancient and boring as Mr. Gully, always going on and on about the trip she'd taken to Athens in 1927; and Mr. Calvin, the geography teacher, never let up on how he'd won the war against the Japs in New Guinea. But no one read comics or played noughts-and-crosses in their lessons, no one talked loudly or moved around the room. Mr. Gully just wasn't a proper teacher. Everything about him was wrong.

His dust coat, for instance. It came down to his ankles and was stiff as cardboard—not with starch, like the other science master, Mr. Langford's, but with plain dirt. The stains on it didn't vanish like Mr. Langford's did, over the weekend; they just stayed there until they were overlaid by new ones. The coat didn't smell, but 1D pretended it did, holding their noses as Mr. Gully passed by their desks.

He had all kinds of disgusting habits. When he talked, when he went on about his boring old force pumps, or even when he delivered his customary, embarrassing greeting at the start of each lesson, he blew little beads of spit out of his blubbery lips: Foaming at the mouth, 1D called it, and the kids in the front row always pretended to duck when he spoke, or ostentatiously wiped a sleeve or an arm. He burped frequently—quiet burps, it was true, but still. . . . And Ella Price claimed she'd seen him once, at the tap by the side of the library verandah, actually *spewing* down the drain. Right in public! Imagine that! Couldn't even be bothered going up to the toilet. Next thing he'd be pissing himself in class. *Ugh!*

The most irritating thing of all was the way he didn't really seem to be *there*, half the time. In the middle of a lesson he'd often stop halfway through a sentence to gaze out of the window, his mouth drooping open, the usual spit beads lolling at the corners, his eyes staring right out of his head, at *nothing*. For there was no one out there (they all craned their necks to see)—not a thing was going on outside the window except rain. And before the rain had begun, sun or cloud, but never anything worth looking at.

He did it sometimes when he was writing on the board: stopping suddenly, jaw dropping, eyes goggling straight at the wall, like a wino with a fit of the horrors.

"What's up, sir?" Jimmy Cooney would call, but old Gully never replied. He didn't seem to hear; it was as if at times he lost touch with the world. Or, as 1D's parents might have put it, as though Mr. Gully was a shingle short.

1D played little jokes on him. They would never have
dared to play jokes on anyone else (unless it was April Fools'
Day), though they did get in a bit of practice on the visiting
student teachers. But Mr. Gully didn't blush or burst into
tears like those young things; he was altogether a disap-
pointing victim. When he opened his desk drawer and
found a dead rat inside, he simply pretended it wasn't there.
When he sat down and found his chair wet, he just rose
stiffly to his feet, took a grubby old snot rag out of his
pocket, and wiped it dry. When, writing on the board, he
discovered the chalk squeaked because it had been dipped
in water at both ends, he just tried another stick, and another, and when he found they were all wet, he patiently
sorted through his pockets until he found a spare, dry stick
of his own.

This terrible patience enraged 1D—nothing seemed to
rouse the old coot, and they were fast running out of tricks.
There weren't so many jokes you could play in a portable
classroom; and during those gloomy long days of rain, with
so many teachers staying safe and snug at the top of the
hill, so many free periods, 1D racked their brains for new
ones. It was difficult, for you had to be careful—anything
really dangerous, like a trip rope across the doorway or a
brick balanced above it, was out—because if old Gully was
injured, then the other teachers would be sure to find out.
Even something fairly modest, like the rattling envelope
trick, was out: Glenys Styles had played that one on an
uncle and he'd fainted right away. He'd had a bad heart,
too. Old Gully looked like he might have a bad heart; his
face was sometimes a peculiar gray color. You couldn't actually *kill* someone.

Then Juliet Miller told them about the program she'd
seen on television a few nights back. Juliet was the only

kid in the class who had a big-screen television. She was different in other ways too: Her father was a doctor, and she'd lived on the North Shore and even gone to a posh private school. Juliet was posh herself—you could tell just by her voice, and the kids in 1D were a bit wary of her.

But Juliet was taking care of that; already her accent was changing, and in those wild free periods with the rain streaming on and on down the windows, she was the noisiest kid of all.

Now, sitting on the teacher's table, swinging her skinny legs in their black stockings, waving her arms, she commanded silence while she gave 1D the gist of the TV play.

"A man woke up one morning," she began, "on a perfectly ordinary day, and he— he found that everyone was using different words."

"What do you mean?"

"Well, you know—instead of saying 'Good morning,' his wife and kids said 'Good row,' and then, at his office, and in the street, everyone was saying it: 'Good row.' "

"Good *row?*"

"Yes—they all used a different word. 'Row' instead of 'morning.' "

"Sounds screwy to me," objected Jimmy Cooney, "and I don't see how—"

Juliet ignored him and hurried on. "And when he asked why they were saying 'row' all the time, they didn't know what he was talking about; they just thought he was queer, you know, mental—because 'row' was the right word for them. It *meant* morning. See? And it built up—every day more and more words changed, so that soon he couldn't understand what anyone was saying."

"What happened in the end?"

"Well"—Juliet hesitated, blinking her eyes behind their

thick glasses. She didn't really know what had happened, as she'd been packed off to bed well before the end of the play. But she could make a good guess, and as they hadn't seen the program, her classmates couldn't catch her out. Unless one of them knew someone who had seen . . . she hesitated again, blinking ferociously.

"Well?"

"Come on, four eyes, tell us what happened!"

Juliet flushed. "He went *mad*. They shut him up in a lunatic asylum with big high walls."

1D was silent.

"You can't imagine how spooky it was," Juliet went on. "Not the asylum, but when all the people were using the wrong words. It sounded really *strange*."

"But I don't see what all that's got to do with playing tricks on Gully," interrupted Elaine Quinn, a tall, tight-lipped girl who would one day become matron of Summer Hill Girls' Home. She stood with her arms folded across her narrow chest and eyed Juliet with sharp suspicion. Juliet was far too la-di-da for Elaine's liking.

"But don't you see," cried Juliet. "We could—" she swallowed excitedly, "we could use it on him. You know, change the words when we spoke to him. Just one word to start with, a word you use a lot, like 'is' or 'the.' I bet it'd really shake him."

1D was silent, considering this idea. At first sight the plan seemed tame, and complicated too, but when they tried out a few sentences, they found that Juliet was right: The effect was surprisingly spooky, even when you knew what was going on. And old Gully wouldn't.

"What if he's seen your famous show?" asked Elaine. "Or someone's told him about it?"

For a moment Juliet was disconcerted, but some of the

other kids burst out laughing. "Can you *imagine* old Gully watching a movie like that?" choked Martin Kingston.

Everyone except Elaine giggled with relief. Of course he wouldn't; he was too old-fashioned. He probably didn't even have a TV.

"But someone might have *told* him," insisted Elaine.

Jimmy Cooney scotched even that, reminding them that you never saw Gully in the staff room: He ate his lunch with Mr. Langford in the little room behind the science lab. "And Langford *hates* TV; he'd never have seen it," he said.

So they tried it. They began as Juliet had suggested, using only one word. At first Mr. Gully didn't seem to notice the substitution, but this wasn't so surprising; it was the way he always acted, no matter what they did. Only sharp-eyed Glenys Styles caught the little flicker of his wrinkly gray eyelids that gave him away.

Then they tried two words, and it was astonishing what a difference this made. A simple sentence, with the words carefully chosen, took on the appearance almost of another language. It *sounded* familiar, because some of the words were unchanged, but when you tried to make out the sentence and found that it was strangely meaningless, well, even Patty Clunes, a plump, placid girl who spent the free periods knitting baby jackets for her sisters' kids, said it gave her the creeps. And the rain falling down outside and the queer brown gloom in the room added to the spookiness, the queer sense of being at the *end* of something.

At first, with just one word changed, and even with two, Mr. Gully had been able to work out the basic meaning of their questions, and after a longish silence he'd reel out the answer with that curious, faraway expression on his face, as if there was nothing unusual going on. But as they

changed three words, and even four, his difficulties in-
creased: he sat there gaping, gobs of spittle appearing at
the corners of his mouth, while the questioners waited,
standing politely beside their desks as they'd never done
before for Mr. Gully.

"Sir?" they'd gently prompt him. And Mr. Gully sat still
as a rock in his chair, except for his hands, which twiddled
hopelessly with the catches of his old brown suitcase. With
a stagey sigh and a face full of mock puzzlement, the ques-
tioner would sit down at his desk and another would rise
to his feet. "Sir?" They spoke pleasantly, naturally—for
that was the trick, Juliet had informed them. You had to
act completely normal.

And after a time, though it was a very long time, halfway
through the second week of the torment of Mr. Gully, the
old science teacher did react. He struggled up from his
chair, slow and stiff as usual, and walked to the door. Fumbling at the catch, he plucked it open, and then for a moment seemed to waver, like a person lost under water,
before shambling suddenly across to the edge of the verandah. There, sticking his head out over the edge, he
spewed onto the ground beneath, emitting a thin, trans-
lucent stream of bile, shot with little silver bubbles like
the slime from a crushed snail. He straightened, and it hung
from his gaping mouth in gleaming, viscous threads that
swung slowly to and fro with the movement of his harsh
breathing. 1D, who had crowded to the door to see what
happened next, drew back in horror.

Old Gully shambled off in the rain. Although they didn't
rush to the windows to watch, they couldn't help but see
him, couldn't stop their eyes from straying to the glass,
through which they saw, some moments later, the gray dust-
coated figure, crumpled somehow, as if there was no one

inside the familiar garment, slowly climbing the steps in the rain.

"He left his umbrella," whispered Juliet.

"And his port of pumps," added Jimmy. This was somehow horrifying. They all stared at the old brown case left open there on the desk, the glass pumps lying neatly side by side, gleaming and glistening against the gloom.

Juliet began to cry. Various girls clustered around and patted her on the back.

"It wasn't *your* fault," whispered Patty Clunes. "It couldn't have been that—no one spews up just because someone's having a bit of a joke. It wasn't us."

"Anyway, he's always burping," put in Glenys Styles. "And remember that time Ella saw him spewing outside the library. Didn't you, Ella?"

Ella Price nodded fiercely.

"He's probably got an ulcer or something," suggested Martin Kingston.

"Nerves of the stomach," said Elaine Quinn briskly. "My mother's got them; she can't keep anything down."

It wasn't nerves of the stomach. What it really was, no one in 1D could be certain, because Mr. Langford, the science master, shouted so loud they were too scared to take anything in. "Forty years of teaching thankless, vicious little sods like you lot," he roared, "and what does he get for it? That damned bloody incubus gnawing his guts out—" Mr. Langford's face was deathly pale, his eyes glittered and tears spilled out of them; he didn't even bother to wipe them away. He could find no words to describe 1D, he said, no words at all. "I wish," he shouted, "I wish—" but what he wished they never found out, for slamming shut the port of pumps, grabbing the old black umbrella, he made off into the rain.

They were quiet when he was gone. In the silence the rain drummed louder than ever and the brown gloom seemed to thicken and swirl before their eyes. The smell of wet wool was suffocating.

"What's an incubus?" asked Patty Clunes suddenly.

No one seemed to know. Then Juliet whispered, "I *think* I know what it is. There was this play on television— science fiction—where these, these *things*, like seeds, came down from outer space, and people swallowed them, and they grew, from the *inside*—"

Jimmy Cooney turned on her sharply. "Shut up!" he barked.

Ella Price screamed. "I'm never going to watch television, never, never!" she vowed, and burst into noisy crying.

Then there was silence again. And each of them thought how, when old Gully came back, they'd make it up to him: They'd be quiet and pay attention, they'd read up the textbook and do their assignments and pass well in the exams. No more talking and reading comics and playing games. No more jokes.

Only Mr. Gully never came back.

Mr. Pepper

When Hettie woke up in her hotel room that first morning, she thought, just for a second, that she was at home. It was easy enough to do, for the door and window were in exactly the same place as they were in her own room at home. But nothing else was the same. The hotel furniture was new and glossy, there was a telephone by her bed, and the wide window, behind its tall, swishing curtains, gave a long view of the esplanade and the smooth sea washing in behind the pines.

Hettie loved having a room of her own in that grand hotel: She felt grown up and independent, even though her parents were just in the room next door. And it was surprising how quickly and completely her old, familiar life dropped away: the house in Curlew Street, school, Tuesday-afternoon piano lessons with Mrs. Casamento—even her best friends, Natalie and Tess. It was almost as if Nat and Tess had never existed at all, and she even felt she wouldn't really care if she never saw them anymore. When this thought came to her, walking down the esplanade, she felt a twinge of guilt: Tess and Nat were her oldest friends; she'd shared all her secrets with them. And she hurried into the souvenir shop on the corner and chose the two prettiest postcards she could find to send to them.

But back in her room, she couldn't think of anything to write, not even a single sentence to fill in the tiny space on the back of the picture. *Wish you were here:* that was what people wrote on postcards. But she didn't—she didn't really wish Nat and Tess were here; she liked being on her own, walking the seaside streets in her bright new summer clothes, eating dinner in the hotel dining room with her parents, pretending they were a couple of elegant strangers she'd just met in the hotel foyer.

And then, two days before the holiday ended, Hettie had a nightmare. She dreamed she woke up in her shabby old room at home, with the faded print curtains swinging faintly in the breeze, and her own face, when she sat up in bed, reflected in the mirror of her dressing table.

She'd woken because she'd heard a noise: the racketty whir of her mother's sewing machine coming quite distinctly from the small room down the hall. Hettie glanced at the clock on her bedside table: It was three o'clock in the morning—why was her mother sewing *now?* There was something scary in the very idea. She got out of bed and tiptoed down the hall. The sewing-room door was closed, and there was no light showing from beneath. Hettie was even more frightened: How could her mother be sewing in the dark?

She pushed the door open; the window blinds were up and moonlight shone through, enough moonlight for Hettie to see quite clearly the figure hunched over the machine, pushing wads of thick, dark fabric beneath the flashing needle. It was a little old man, with a shiny domed skull and great bushy white eyebrows. He looked up at Hettie, and his small black eyes glistened; then he smiled: a long, quiet, gloating smile. "I li-ike you," he sang, in a small, high voice that had a little whistle in it.

This was so terrible to Hettie that she opened her mouth to scream, and when no scream came rushing up from her bursting lungs, she felt she might die—and then she woke up and found herself lying in her comfortable hotel bed. Just to be sure, she got up and looked out of the window. Yes, there was the esplanade, empty in the moonlight, and the sea glittering behind the pines. She sighed with relief and crawled back into bed, though she didn't want to go to sleep, not right away, in case the dream came back.

As she lay there, Hettie became aware of a sound: a low, racketty whiring, rising and falling, going on and on. She listened for what seemed like hours, panic tightening her throat, just as it had in the dream when she hadn't been able to scream, and then, as dawn broke and light began to rim the windows, she realized what the sound was. Not Mr. Pepper at his sewing machine, but just someone snoring on the other side of the wall, in the next room. She smiled to herself—that was it, of course—she'd heard the snoring through her sleep, and it had turned itself into a dream, become Mr. Pepper at his sewing machine.

Mr. Pepper! Where had that name come from? She didn't know; it had simply flown into her head. It suited the little man perfectly: It was his without doubt. She shivered. How creepy he had been, and how hateful it was when he'd sung those words to her: "I li-ike you." What right had he to like her? But he was gone, and she was sure, now she knew the sound to be nothing more than her neighbor snoring, that the dream wouldn't come back. The snoring was comforting in its homeliness, even though the little whistle in it reminded her a bit of Mr. Pepper's voice.

"How did you sleep?" the maid asked next morning when she brought in Hettie's pot of tea.

"I kept waking up," replied Hettie. She giggled. "The man in the next room was snoring all night."

"Your father," smiled the maid.

"Oh, no, my father doesn't snore. It was here, in that room," she tapped the wall beside her bed.

"No one in there," said the maid.

"What do you mean?"

"The room's empty. Has been for ages—it's being redecorated." She lowered her voice and added, "There was a fire."

"But I *heard* snoring."

"You must have dreamt it," said the maid. "People dream a lot in this place."

Had she dreamt it? The question bothered Hettie all day. She supposed it was possible—she might have fallen asleep and had another of those dreams where it seemed as if you were awake. The snoring had sounded very real, and the hotel room had seemed real, but then so had Mr. Pepper, hunched over his sewing machine.

She didn't go out on her own that day; she sat on the beach with her parents, trying to read and staring out over the sea. It looked cold.

"Weather's turning," remarked her father. "I wouldn't be surprised if it rained tomorrow."

"And we'll be home," said her mother. "I can't say I'll be sorry, really. I didn't get a wink of sleep last night, and the other nights were almost as bad."

"Why?" asked Hettie eagerly. "Did you hear someone snoring?"

"Snoring?" her mother laughed. "No, I wish I had. It's

just so noisy at night: people coming and going at all hours, banging doors, shouting good night and then, just when you think it's all over, there's that wretched milk cart unloading outside in the yard.''

Hettie frowned. She'd been awake for hours last night and she hadn't heard any of those sounds: no footsteps, no cheery party voices, no rattle of crates as the milk cart unloaded. She'd have been glad of them.

"I'll be thankful to be home in my own bed," sighed her mother.

"So shall I," breathed Hettie.

In the night, the snoring came back again. She woke and heard it: that long, whistling intake of breath, the pause, and then the racketty, monotonous whiring, over and over again. She tapped on the wall, but the snoring went on. She switched on the light. The room sprang brightly into view: the smart new paint, the glossy furniture, the phone by the bed—it was all real, nothing dreamlike about it. She slid out of bed and crossed to the other side of the room. She put her ear to the wall just in case it really was her father; perhaps the change of place, the new bed, the sea air, had turned him into a snorer. But there was no sound from behind that wall. She went back to bed and tried to read, but the words made no sense to her. She kept thinking, What if it's Mr. Pepper? What if he was in that room, behind the wall, a few inches away from her, hunched over his sewing machine, pushing the dark wads of cloth under the needle, faster and faster, senselessly. No, it couldn't be—Mr. Pepper was just a nightmare. That was all.

Perhaps the maid had been mistaken about the room's emptiness. Or the redecorating might have been finished today, and someone had moved in. There was only one way to find out. Wrapping her dressing gown around her, Hettie went out into the hall. The door of the next room was slightly open, and the snoring, she noticed, had ceased.

"Is anyone there?" she whispered, feeling slightly foolish. She pushed the door gently and felt for the light switch: She saw a room full of ladders and paint cans, with the carpet rolled back and shrouded in plastic. The maid had been right; there was no one here, not even, she thought with a sense of relief, Mr. Pepper.

She lay awake all night, waiting for the snoring to begin again. It didn't, though she thought she could make out, faintly, a tiny, breathy, whistling sound. Toward morning, when she heard the cheerful, ordinary noise of the milk crates being unloaded in the yard outside, Hettie fell asleep.

Tess called up on the evening of their return. At the sound of her voice, crackling happily over the wire, Hettie felt her old life taking hold again. How could she have forgotten Tess and Natalie, even felt for a little while that she wouldn't care if she never saw them again? For a moment, just before Tess hung up, Hettie thought of telling her the story of Mr. Pepper, or at least about the snoring that wasn't there. Tess would laugh—or would she? Perhaps she wouldn't—perhaps she'd say, "Oh, Hettie, how *creepy*!" and then Hettie would be scared all over again, she'd begin to feel there might just have been something in it, more than a dream or a simple trick of sound. For that was what she'd decided it must have been: some kind of echo, a sound funneled through the walls of the hotel—through the air vents, perhaps. It seemed odd now, back home, to think how scared she'd been. But she didn't want to risk this sense of security, not just yet, so she didn't tell Tess.

Later, perhaps—some Friday night when she and Natalie were sleeping over and they were telling scary stories in the dark.

How good it was to be back in her own bed, in her own room! And how good it was, later, to wake up and hear nothing at all but the old familiar sounds: the big clock ticking in the hall, the hum of the refrigerator from the kitchen, and, way down the street, Mrs. Hunter's dog barking at the moon. She snuggled deep into the blankets, sighing with happiness. Tomorrow she and Tess and Natalie were going into town: They'd look around the shops and see a movie. . . . Then she heard it. Louder, by far, than it had been in the hotel, louder and closer, right up beside her in the wall: the long, rising breath, the little whistle, and then the deep, rattling whir.

Hettie sat up in bed and began to cry. She cried and cried, as she hadn't done since she was a very small child. And then she stopped. For someone had spoken.

"Don't cry" came Mr. Pepper's high, whistly voice beside her. "Don't cry, little Hettie—I li-ike you."

Last Strawberries

I n mid-March the clocks are put back and the sun
slides down behind the hilly suburbs a little after
seven. Summer vanishes all at once, the gardens are filled
with dusk and shadow, and the children stay inside. Lights
are switched on early.

It's sad, Eleanor thinks as she stands by the kitchen
bench, shelling peas for dinner and watching the sunset
through the windows. The clouds are bright crimson, like
cotton wool dipped in cochineal. It's like a death, like
something going that won't ever come back.

It seems strange to have darkness falling when it's still
so warm, as if the day isn't really finished at all, but someone's put a stop to it, like throwing a blanket over a bird-
cage. It's still warm enough to wear a cotton skirt and T-
shirt and not feel cold, yet Eleanor shivers suddenly. She's
a tall girl with long dark hair and big brown glossy eyes,
not yet twenty-two. She married young, straight out of
fourth form, and inside her head she still feels exactly the
same age as that day when she went into the vice principal's
office to get her exit papers. Sixteen. "You're making a big

mistake," the vice principal said coldly, and Eleanor had laughed.

Stupid old idiot *he* was, she thinks now, smiling to herself—and then the darkness outside catches her up again. "Sad," she whispers, switching her gaze quickly from the windows to her small daughter, Nell, crouched on the carpet with a wooden jigsaw, a farmyard scene where the animals, horse and cow and pig and goat, fit into holes cut into their exact shapes, like shadows. As Nell struggles to fit the horse into the cow's shadow, Eleanor has an idea; it's an impulse, really, coming quick and bright like a flash in her head. She will slip down to the supermarket and get strawberries; they will have them with cream for dessert: the last strawberries of the season, in memory of summer. Eleanor picks up her car keys and hurries out onto the terrace.

A voice follows her; she looks back and sees Nell standing at the screen door. "I want to come," calls the child. "I want to come with you." Eleanor is halfway up the drive now, heading toward the yellow Renault parked outside in the street. She hesitates; she doesn't want to take Nell, she wants to be quick, she wants to get the strawberries and bring them back home. Nell will hold her up, pulling at her skirt, wanting to look at the toys, pestering her to buy things.

"You stay with Daddy," she calls. "I'm just going to the supermarket. I won't be a minute. I just want to get some strawberries."

Eleanor is lucky. There is just one punnet left in the store, and even after the long day on the shelves, the strawberries are perfect: ripe and juicy, a clear scarlet, glistening faintly, bright like blood. They are very expensive, a dollar ninety-nine instead of fifty cents. Because they're almost

out of season, thinks Eleanor. Next week they'll be gone
for good. She reaches for the little box quickly, before
someone else can take them, and hurries to the checkout.
There's a new woman at the till; Eleanor hasn't seen her
before. And, waiting her turn in the queue, glancing
around, she notices that there are new operators at all four
checkouts. It must be the evening shift, she thinks. And
then it's her turn, and the new woman wraps the strawberries in plastic and counts out the change.

"Have a good day," she says. The phrase is new to
Eleanor. She frowns slightly; it seems an odd thing to say,
with the dark coming on, and the way the woman says it
is strange too, brisk and mechanical, like a parrot who's
been taught to talk.

In the street outside Eleanor recognizes someone—Mrs.
Hiller, the mother of one of Nell's kindergarten friends.
She almost *doesn't* recognize her, for Mrs. Hiller has
changed since Eleanor saw her last. Terribly. She looks ten
years older at least; her cheeks are sunk, her skin is wrinkled, her hair is thickly snaggled with gray. Eleanor is
shocked out of speech; a greeting dies on her lips. How
long is it since she last saw Mrs. Hiller? Surely not long at
all—at the kindergarten fête, four months back. What has
happened to her—some grief, some terrible loss?

On the pavement, in the lamplight, Eleanor struggles to
speak before it is too late. "Hullo," she says at last. Mrs.
Hiller has already passed by, but she hears, and turns at
the sound of Eleanor's voice. Turns and stares, rather va-
cantly, wrinkling her brow in puzzlement, as if she now
has difficulty in recognizing Eleanor. "Hullo," she replies,
but in a bright, rather false tone, the kind you use for
strangers who speak up unexpectedly in the street. People
you've forgotten. And she hurries on, quickly.

Crossing the road to the car park, clutching her strawberries, Eleanor feels a sudden wash of panic. Perhaps *she* has aged too, over the summer, become so old looking that Mrs. Hiller doesn't know who she is. Breathing deeply, she stifles an urge to run to the red-brick rest rooms beside the service station, to peer into the cloudy, rust-specked mirror and check on her face. She *could* look older; she doesn't spend much time at the mirror these days. And they say getting old is like that: It happens *suddenly* . . . and she'll be twenty-two this year, no longer a girl. But surely Nell would tell her—kids notice things like that. She'd say, "Your skin's gone all wrinkly," or "You've got some white hairs, Mum."

Eleanor won't look—not now. She won't be so silly, won't run into that awful gloomy rest room, won't even look in the car rear-vision mirror. She'll wait till she gets home, till dinner is over and the strawberries are eaten. Perhaps by then the panic will have subsided and she won't even bother. After all, she's only twenty-one. Ridiculous to think of being old! Mrs. Hiller might have been ill; there's a bad flu going about. Perhaps when Eleanor sees her next, she'll look young again, except for the gray hair.

She drives west down Carrum Avenue, toward the intersection with City Road. A little beyond that, up the hill, is her home. Through the windscreen, out beyond the jumble of trees and rooftops, she can see the moon rising, a sharp, new, silver one, with a cold, bright star beside it. It's a long time since she's seen a new moon rise, ages really—yet even as this thought passes through her mind, there comes a feeling of familiarity so intense it's like oppression: as if every single evening, for years and years, she's seen the new moon rising with a cold, bright star beside it.

She drives on, nearing home, and then suddenly, at a corner just before the intersection, she turns off into a narrow side street, and then into another, and so, by a slow, winding route, she returns to the car park and the supermarket. She hurries inside, straight to the fruit section at the back of the shop, and reaches for the very last punnet of strawberries. At the checkout counter she notices the new operators and is given the curious, parrotlike greeting she doesn't remember hearing before: "Have a good day." In the street outside she meets Mrs. Hiller, is shocked by the change in her and afraid that she, too, might be getting old, unrecognizable. She drives down Carrum Avenue and sees the new moon rising, and the cold bright star beside it, feels again that heavy familiarity that is like oppression—and turns off once more at the small side street before the intersection, and goes on, by the same circular route, to the supermarket.

As she always does, over and over, day by day and year by year in an evening that is always the first true one of autumn, with the crimson clouds piling up like cotton wool and the new moon and the bright, cold star rising, and the last punnet of summer strawberries on the front seat of the old-fashioned yellow Renault.

At her house across the intersection there are people in the kitchen whom Eleanor might find barely recognizable. Her husband's hair is gray, grayer even than Mrs. Hiller's. His wife Jane sits at the kitchen table shelling peas into a white china bowl. Her smooth hair shines in the light—blond like Nell's, like her husband's, when he was younger. They are a family of blonds now.

Nell, fourteen years old and tall like her mother, opens the fridge door and finds the strawberries that Jane bought that morning, plump and red and faintly glistening, like blood. "Strawberries!" she cries—and across the room her father says simply, "Oh, *Nell*." Mixed with the sadness in his voice there is a faint edge of exhausted irritation, as if he is tired to death of this word.

And Nell sees again her mother's face, eager and excited and flushed with the last pink of the cotton-wool clouds. "I just want to get some strawberries," she calls as she races up the driveway toward the car. "I won't be a minute."

The yellow Renault was a write-off.

Aunty Maidie's Starving

I am past fifty now, yet I still live here alone in the old house behind the sand dunes. People say I have a withered hand; a gray, useless hand that feels nothing and cannot move, a hand as small as a child's—that's what people say. *I* say I have no hand.

When I was a young boy, I thought I'd live in the city when I grew up, a city far away from the sea and filled with noise and lights and people. My sister moved away, but I stayed on, working in the township beyond the headland like my father did, riding home by night along the sandy track, my cycle lamp the only light for miles around.

Sometimes on the homeward ride a song runs through my head: "You always hurt . . . the one you love . . . the one you love be-est of all. . . ." Over and over it goes, because I only know those two lines, and I may have got the words wrong, it is all so long ago now.

It was a song my aunty Maidie used to sing in the evenings when we walked together along the beach, in a voice that was thick and slow like warm honey dropping from a spoon. Aunty Maidie was romantic: She liked to watch the light fade and the sun set and the moon come up to make a path across the sea. Sometimes that moon path looked solid as a silver pavement, and she said it was just the place a ghost might walk, coming back home. "They come to those they love best," she whispered, and I knew she was thinking about my uncle Ronnie—that she expected him to come walking toward her from his bed in the sea, though there was no one but herself who believed he'd loved her best.

He had died a few years earlier, swept off the rocks at Blind Man's Point. They'd never found his body, and it was one of my fears that some evening, walking along the sands, we would meet Uncle Ronnie, not gliding toward us, noble and ghostly, on his silver path, but rolled up on the tide line, a stinking bundle of bones and rot, wrapped round in seaweed and slime.

I remembered him well; you don't easily forget a person like that, and the thing I remembered most clearly was how hard and sharp and bony he had been—not thin like my aunty, just hard, like a man made out of flint. And how everyone had hated him.

He drank and wouldn't work, though that would have been forgiven him; there were plenty like that in the township. People hated him because he was cruel to my aunty: He wouldn't let her have children because he didn't like them, and he wouldn't let her have a pet because he said they were nuisances. He left her alone a lot, and the kids at school used to say he had a girlfriend, a lady called Marta Vickers, who lived out at Harper's Crossing—but those kids were always giggling and laughing about someone. I've never liked gossip, not even when I was a child.

I often walked with Aunty Maidie along the sands in the evenings, when there was nothing much else to do. My mother was busy with my new baby sister and my father was always tired after his long day in the factory. And it was during these walks that Aunty Maidie began telling me stories about Uncle Ronnie, stories that I thought of as secrets, because she told them to no one else, but that I knew in my heart were lies. She spoke of kindness: She described how, when she was sick with the flu, Uncle Ronnie would sit beside her bed and read poetry to her.

"He loved poetry," she whispered. "And he knew I loved it too." She sighed. "He always chose exactly the right pieces; he knew my favorites without ever being told."

I didn't believe it for a moment. I'd never seen Uncle Ronnie with a book, and I couldn't imagine him sitting by the bed of a sick person—he hated illness. If you were sick, I thought, then he'd just take off, and he wouldn't come back until you were better and no bother to him. I frowned.

Aunty Maidie saw the frown. "You don't believe me, do you?" she said sadly, and with an odd, sly expression in her dreamy eyes she began singing her favorite song, the one I thought of as hers. "You always hurt . . . the one you love . . . the one you love be-est of all. . . ."

"Yes," I protested. "I do, really. I was frowning at something else."

Secretly I thought her silly, but I felt sad for her; she'd never had anything, never had a good husband like my mother had, or a child of her own to love, or even a house of her own. When Uncle Ronnie was alive, they'd lived in shabby rented rooms in the township, and now that he was dead, she lived in our house, in the long narrow room at the back that was really just an enclosed verandah, drafty in the winter. Even her dresses were old ones of my mother's, and it seemed to me they always had been. She wanted me to believe her stories, and I felt that believing them was like giving her something, so I pretended. But I was uneasy.

Once she showed me a brooch that she said my uncle had given her the day they first met. It was a cheap thing, tawdry, a small bunch of flowers molded in paste, with sprinkles of fairy glitter embedded in the petals. I knew she was lying—they hadn't had fairy glitter back in those days she was talking about, and I'd seen those brooches in the new Woolworths that had just opened in the township. Some instinct told me she had stolen it; I could imagine her so clearly, slipping it into the pocket of her old tweed coat, and the swift sliding movement of her big dark eyes.

After these storytelling sessions on the beach, when we were back in the warm house and Aunty Maidie had gone to bed in her narrow room, I'd suddenly feel icy cold, and I'd go and stand up close beside my mother as she rocked the baby to sleep before the fire. Sometimes she sang the song "You always hurt . . . the one you love—"

"Don't sing that song," I begged her. "It's Aunty Maidie's."

"Songs don't belong to anyone."

"Yes, they do. And anyway, it's not *true*."

"How do you mean?"

"Well, it's not true, is it? You *don't* always hurt the one you love—you wouldn't hurt Jenny, would you?"

My mother lifted her head and looked at me. "Or you, Rolly," she said.

I flung my arms around her and she gave me a quick hug, and I drew back a little, feeling guilty because Aunty Maidie had no one to hug her or keep her warm.

When she showed me the brooch again, I drew in my breath in mock rapture. "It's beautiful," I breathed. "He must have loved you awfully."

"He loved me best," she said proudly. "I know he seemed harsh sometimes, but that was because— because of what happened to him as a child."

"What was that?" I asked. It wasn't easy to think of Uncle Ronnie as a child.

"His mother died and his father married again, when poor Ronnie was only—" she hesitated, glanced at me, and continued, "when he was only nine, like you. And the new stepmother didn't like him. She made his father send him away to live with his cousins at Deniliquin. They weren't bad boys, those cousins, only rude and rough and thoughtless, and they made fun of Ronnie because he was small and weak, and every night he cried himself to sleep on his little pillow. He never forgot those days. It made him hard sometimes, but he didn't mean it."

I pondered this story. It was hard to believe; it sounded so much like a fairy tale, with its cruel stepmother and the tiny boy being cast out among strangers. That night, when Aunty Maidie had gone to her room, I asked my parents if the story was true.

My father frowned. "That old tale," he muttered crossly, glancing across at my mother.

"Is it true?"

He didn't answer. He told me to go to bed, and through the open doors I heard them talking in snatches here and there. "Morbid," my father muttered. "Unhappy," said my mother. "Hospital . . . treatment," my father replied. "No good will come from all this walking on the beach," he pronounced.

But there wasn't much more walking by the sea, for that winter Aunty Maidie died. She caught cold walking in the sand hills in the early morning before anyone was awake. I found her there myself, when I was out before breakfast looking for old Smokey, who'd broken her hobble at night and wandered off. I found the cow way over near the estuary, nibbling at the tough green grass that always made her sick. And on my way back through the sand hills I came upon Aunty Maidie: She was kneeling in a hollow beside a mass of those big purple-blue flowers that grew everywhere around our place.

"Look," she cried when she saw me, holding out the flowers. She'd twisted them into a rough circle.

"Convolvulus," I murmured. "Pretty." I saw that she was wearing only her nightie, with nothing warm on top.

"Morning glory," she corrected me.

"You shouldn't be out here in the cold," I said. "There are flowers like that at home. There's some growing around the tank stand."

"Morning glory," she repeated. "He made me a wreath of it, to wear in my hair. I had lovely hair in those days, pure black, and it came down to my waist." She put a hand up to her brief gray curls: My mother trimmed them for her with the kitchen shears, on the first Tuesday of every month. "You did really like him, didn't you?" Aunty Maidie asked in a small voice.

I was silent.

"Just a little bit?" she pleaded, with a queer, jerky smile.

"Oh, lots, lots," I blurted, sick inside.

She laughed joyfully. "He loved me best and I loved him best, but now that he's gonè, it's you I love best. It's you I'll come to."

"Let's go home, Aunty," I cried, feeling afraid. "I've got to milk Smokey."

She died quite simply in her narrow bed, the inflammation closing up her lungs before the doctor could be fetched. She looked just asleep, lying there beneath the counterpane, but when I bent to kiss her cheek it was cold and rubbery, like kelp on the shore, and I knew Aunty Maidie had already turned into something else.

"She didn't want to live," my mother sighed. "Poor Maidie."

"Will she come back?" I asked.

"Come back? What do you mean?"

"Like a ghost. She said she would. She said she'd come back for the one she loved best—that's me."

"Don't be silly," said my mother. "There are no such things as ghosts."

"Dead is dead," said my father, who was standing behind us in the doorway. He never spoke much, so when he did, you listened.

Now I walked on the beach by myself in the evenings, watching the moon come up and the stars breaking out of the darkening sky. There was never anyone about, we were so far from the township; and it suddenly struck me what a mournful place we lived in, with only the sound of the sea and the wind rustling in the grasses and no light anywhere but the one burning from our tiny house, and I thought that when I grew up, I'd move to the city and live among noise and lights and people. Sometimes as I walked, I imagined I heard my aunty's voice behind me, heavy and sweet, singing the same old song. But when I looked around, there was no one there. "Dead is dead," my father had said, and I was glad of it.

And then one night, a month or so after her death, I heard Aunty Maidie singing in the garden. The voice was clear and high, quite different from what it had been, but I knew it was her because of the song.

I jumped out of bed and ran to the window, and I saw her standing on the little patch of grass beside the tank stand. The dawn light was coming, that faint, gray, luminous light like the pearly shell of an oyster, and I saw that she had flowers in her hand, the blue convolvulus that she always called morning glory. She was ripping them up, rending and tearing and stuffing the pieces in her mouth.

"Aunty Maidie!" I cried, horrified.

She turned toward me, shreds of blue petals stuck to her lips and chin. She'd always been thin, but now her thinness was extraordinary and terrible, like those pictures of prisoners in concentration camps that my mother always hid from me. Her head was big and trembled wildly on her frail neck.

"Ah, Rolly!" she called. "My darling Rolly!" I climbed over the sill and walked across the cold, stubby grass. In the distance I heard Smokey bellowing and was glad of the sound.

"I'm hungry," Aunty Maidie whispered as I came up close to her. "I'm hungry, Rolly—get me something to eat or I'll starve."

I stared at her and I shook all over. My mouth wouldn't open to speak.

"I'm starving, Rolly," she repeated. "And I love you best."

I turned and fled into the house, down the hall toward the kitchen. The fire was dead, but there was a plate of pumpkin scones on the table, left over from supper. I seized them and ran back to the tank stand. Aunty Maidie grabbed the scones from me and gobbled them greedily, and then she dashed the plate to the ground and it flew up in shatters. I stared in amazement: I had never seen her do anything like this; she had always been soft and pale and quiet.

She clutched at me. "It's not enough!" she cried. "Not

enough. I must have more. Give me *more*!" Her fingers, sharp and clawlike, tore into my hand—they burned like hot pincers. She thrust her big head down toward me. "Let me go!" I cried. "Let me go!" And as I screamed, the sun began to rise over the sand hills, red and bold and bringing daylight. "I'm starving!" Aunty Maidie cried again, and vanished.

I ran to my parents' room. "Aunty Maidie's starving!" I shouted. "She was in the garden, by the tank stand, eating flowers. I gave her some scones, but I couldn't give her enough, and she hurt my hand. Look! Look!" I thrust my hand toward them—the angry red marks were burned deep into the flesh.

"Shhh," said my mother. "Hush, you'll wake Jenny."

"My hand!" I screamed.

"There's nothing wrong with your hand, darling," said my mother, pressing it gently. "You've had a bad dream. That's all."

"But there are red marks, red marks!"

"There's nothing," she said, and I could tell by her puzzled, anxious expression that she couldn't see the marks at all. "You must try not to think so much of Aunty Maidie, Rolly," she said softly.

"But she's starving. She was in the garden, eating those blue—"

"Hush," said my mother. "Forget. Go to sleep."

"Dead is dead," said my father.

Though no one could see them, those marks stayed on my hand, and when I lay in bed at night, listening for Aunty Maidie's voice in the garden, they throbbed and burned. She loved me best, I thought, and I wished that she had hated me. I wished I had been mean to her when she lived, that I had never listened to her secrets, never pretended that I had believed them or that I had liked Uncle Ronnie. Then she would not have come to me.

Four days from the first visit I woke again and heard her singing. It was dark outside; all I could see in the garden was the faint white blur of her dress beside the tank stand. I kept quiet, but the window was open a little, and she heard me breathing. The white dress fluttered.

"Rolly!" she cried. "Rolly, I'm starving. Bring me something, I need to have something. I *must*." She came up close and placed one of her clawlike hands upon the sill.

"Go away!" I cried. "I haven't got anything for you."

She fixed me with her deep dark eyes. She was different, I saw. It wasn't just that she was thinner; there was something cruel and hard in her, the flintlike quality that had been in my Uncle Ronnie when he was alive. She was cruel and cared for no one. And I wondered if my uncle, down beneath the sea, had changed also and become pale and soft and quiet.

Aunty Maidie grabbed my hand. She jerked it up toward her narrow face, opened her mouth, and gobbled it down. There was nothing left: just my wrist at the end of the pajama sleeve, and a pain like fire. She seized my other hand but I dragged it back and ran toward the middle of the room. Her face loomed at the window—there was blood on her lips, trickling down her chin. Both her hands were on the sill now; she was getting ready to climb into the room. I ran into the hall and at once I saw that it wasn't late at all, for the kitchen door was open and my parents sat inside playing cards at the table while Jenny slept beside the fire in her baby basket.

"She's taken my hand!" I screamed. "Aunty Maidie has taken my hand!"

My mother pulled me on her lap. She took my good hand and the bleeding stump; she stroked them both as if they were the same. "Your hands are fine, Rolly," she said. "They are good, strong little hands, but if you like, we'll go to the doctor tomorrow and he can look at them."

"She's taken my hand," I sobbed, "because she was starving and had nothing and because she loved me best. Because I listened to her secrets and—"

"Shhh," said my mother, stroking my hair. "Quiet."

Then I looked across the room. The window here was open a little because of the fire's heat, and outside I saw Aunty Maidie's face, long and white in the dark. Her lips moved. "*Starving,*" they said.

And suddenly I knew how to make her leave me. I glanced up at my mother, and I calmed myself and spoke softly, so she wouldn't tell me to hush. "Uncle Ronnie was a horrible man, wasn't he?" I asked.

"It doesn't do to speak ill of the dead," she replied.

"Dead is dead," intoned my father. "And let them lie."

"But he was bad. I hated him," I said, louder, looking all the time toward the window. "I hated your Ronnie, Aunty Maidie. He was cruel and hard and wicked, and he hated *you*—he wouldn't let you have children, or new dresses, or a house. He left you alone and—" I remembered the gossip I had heard in the schoolyard "—he didn't love you a bit. He went with Marta Vickers; he used to go to her house at night and sleep in her bed. He had nothing for you, nothing! I never believed about the poetry and the brooch and the flowers and the bad stepmother—I only pretended because you were silly and I felt sorry for you. But I don't anymore—I never loved you either, and I've nothing for you—nothing!"

The face at the window vanished. She went away.

"Dead is dead," I said.

"Go to bed now, Roland," said my father. "You've woken the baby up. Tomorrow we'll take you to the hospital for treatment."

I climbed from my mother's lap and walked slowly back to my room. The window was black and empty, the room was silent, but outside it had begun to rain, a soft rain, like tears falling.